Praise for **S0-AAN-291**

"[A] genuine achievement . . . Mr. McGrath's tales perhaps recall the horror films of Brian DePalma. Not only do they share those movies' baroque romanticism and their tendency to mix up narrative conventions in an expressionistic, post-modern stew, but they also share a similar preoccupation with sex and guilt, violence and death. . . . This young English writer possesses a natural storytelling gift and an ability to invest his narrative with a disturbing psychological subtext."

Michiko Kakutani
The New York Times

"Never before this bewitching book do I remember wanting so badly, like any bobbysoxer, to throw myself at an author's feet. . . . Patrick McGrath deserves widespread admiration and homage. Granted, a collection of stories in which, among other strangenesses, a fly receives his sexual initiation, will not be to all tastes. However, McGrath is inventive enough to offer something for practically anybody who adores offbeat grue."

Michele Slung
Newsday

"Mixing the macabre, the fantastical, the gruesome and the illusionary with a lush and word-loving style, McGrath conjures up an extravagant selection of worlds. . . . With elegance, humor, and respect for the dark side of human nature, McGrath offers polished and entertaining, eminently readable stories."

Publishers Weekly

BLOOD AND WATER
AND OTHER TALES

Patrick McGrath

BALLANTINE BOOKS • NEW YORK

"The Angel" originally appeared in *The Quarterly*; "Lush Triumphant"
and "Hand of a Wanker" in *Between C & D*; "Ambrose Syme"
and "Blood Disease" in *Bomb*; "The Skewer" in *Confrontation*
magazine of Long Island University; "The Boot's Tale" in *New
Observations*; "The E(rot)ic Potato" in the *East Village Eye*; and
"Blood and Water" in *The Missouri Review*.

Library of Congress Catalog Card Number: 87-25667

ISBN 0-345-35585-7

This edition published by arrangement with Poseidon Press, a division
of Simon & Schuster, Inc.

Manufactured in the United States of America

First Ballantine Books Edition: April 1989

For Orshi

Contents

The Angel

You know the Bowery, I presume? It was on the Bowery that I first caught a glimpse of Harry Talboys. I was a writer in those days, and I lived in a five-story walk-up by the men's shelter. I didn't realize at the time that Harry Talboys lived in the same building, though of course I was familiar with the powerful smell of incense that contaminated the lower floors. It was high summer when I met him, high summer in Manhattan, when liquid heat settles on the body of the city like an incubus, and one's whole activity devolves to a languid commerce of flesh and fluids, the ingestion and excretion of the one by the other, and all sane organisms quite simply estivate. I was certainly estivating; I rose late in the day, and after certain minimal ritualistic gestures of the writerly kind made my way to the liquor store. It was on one of these errands, on a garbage-strewn and urine-pungent side-

1

walk, beneath a blazing sun, and slimed in my own sweat, that I first encountered Harry Talboys.

He was making stately progress down the Bowery with a cane. Let me describe him: a tall, thin figure in a seersucker suit the grubbiness of which, the fraying cuffs, the cigarette burns and faded reddish wine stain on the crotch could not altogether disguise the quality of the fabric and the elegance of the cut. Very erect, very tall, very slow, on his head a Panama hat; and his face a veritable atlas of human experience, the nose a great hooked bone of a thing projecting like the prow of a ship, and the mouth—well, the mouth had foundered somewhat, but the old man animated it with lipstick! He must have been at least eighty. His shirt collar was not clean, and he wore a silk tie of some pastel shade—pale lilac or mauve, I seem to remember; and in his buttonhole a fresh white lily. (I never saw Harry Talboys without a fresh flower in his buttonhole.) And as I say, he was making his way down the Bowery, and the men from the men's shelter drinking at the corner of Third Street greeted him warmly. "Hey, Harry!" they called; "Yo, Harry!" and he moved through them with all the graceful condescension of royalty, briefly lifting his Panama to reveal a liver-spotted skull devoid of all but a last few wisps of snow-white hair. Watching this performance I was much taken with the dignity of the old fellow, and with his lipstick. Was there, I asked myself, a story here?

OUR FRIENDSHIP BEGAN WELL: HE ASKED ME INTO HIS apartment for a drink. Such a hot day, he said, hanging up his Panama in the hallway and leaning his stick

2

in the corner; productive activity, he said, was quite out of the question. His accent, to my surprise, was old Boston. (I'm from the North End myself.) The odor of incense was strong, and so was the perfume he wore. He was very liberally scented and smelled, in fact, like an old lady, but there was, I detected it even then, something unpleasant about it, a nuance, a suggestion of overripeness in the bouquet.

Are you familiar with the apartments of the Lower East Side? Designed essentially as holding tanks for wage laborers, they do not err on the side of expansiveness. We entered Harry's living room. Crowded bookshelves, a pair of deep seedy armchairs that faced windows with a clear prospect north to the Chrysler Building, and between the windows, on a rounded, slender-stemmed table of varnished black wood, a vase full of lilies. Directly above the lilies, and between the windows, hung a large crucifix, the body of the Saviour pinned to a cross of white ivory with nailheads of mother-of-pearl. Hanging from the ceiling in the far corner of the room, on a length of copper chain, was the censer whence the fumes emanated. No air conditioner, no fan. There was, however, ice in the kitchen, and Harry made us each a large gin-and-tonic. Then he lowered himself stiffly toward an armchair, the final stage of this operation being a sort of abandoned plunge followed by a long sigh. "Cigarettes," he murmured, rummaging through the pockets of his jacket.

"You have no cats," I said.

"Dreadful creatures," he said. "Can't abide them. Your very good health, Bernard Finnegan!"

We drank. He asked me about my writing. I began to explain, but he quickly lost interest. His gaze shifted to the window, to the glittering blade that the Chrysler Building becomes in the shimmering blue heat of certain summer days. His books impressed me. A good many classical authors—Petronius was represented, Apuleius and Lactantius, and certain of the early Christian writers, Bede and Augustine among others. When I rose to leave, he asked me for my telephone number. Would I, he wondered, have a drink with him again? Yes, I said, with pleasure.

"GIN?"

The censer was, as before, smoldering gently on its chain. It reminded me of my childhood, of chapels and churches in which I had fidgeted through innumerable interminable Masses. Harry's perfume, slightly rotten though it was, one grew accustomed to; not the incense. The stink of it was apparent as soon as one entered the building. I asked him why he burned it.

"Does it disturb you?" he said. He was slicing a lemon on the kitchen counter, very slowly. I was in the other room. The Chrysler Building was glowing in the dusk, and there were red streaks to the west, over the Hudson.

"It makes me feel like a schoolboy."

He looked at me carefully then, those watery blue eyes of his fixing me like a pair of headlights. "Are you a Catholic?" he said.

"Lapsed."

"I too."

He sighed. He became preoccupied. He appeared to be pondering our common connection to the Roman faith. "When I was a young man," he said, when we

4

were settled in our armchairs, "I called myself a Catholic but I lived like a pagan. Oh, I could drink in those days, Bernard! I could drink till dawn. Today, as you see, after one gin I become"—here he smiled with gentle irony—"desperately befuddled. But then! I was happy with my gods, like the ancients. Do you know what we thought the body was, Bernard, back in the Twenties? A temple in which there was nothing unclean. A shrine, to be adorned for the ritual of love! We lived for the moment, Bernard—the purpose of life was to express yourself, and if you were unhappy that was because you were maladjusted, and if you were maladjusted it was because you were repressed. We were excitable, you see, and if there was one thing we would not tolerate"—he turned toward me in his armchair—"it was boredom! Dullness! Anathema!" He gazed off into the night. There was a silence.

"Go on," I said.

"It didn't last. I remember coming back to New York in 1929 . . . My friends all seemed to be dead, or married, or alcoholic . . ." Another pause. "I don't suppose you know the *Rhapsody in Blue?*" He hummed the opening bars, and there was suddenly a tone, in the thickening and aromatic dusk, of intense melancholy, rendered all the more poignant by the slow, faltering cadence of the old man's melody. He said little more that evening, and when I rose to leave he was distant and abstracted. He did apologize, though, for being "such a wretched host."

THE SUMMER PROGRESSED. IN A GIN-BLURRED HEAT HAZE we slipped into August. I spent two or three hours a day at my table and told myself I was working. In fact I made several verbal sketches of Harry Talboys; to what use I would put them I had no clear idea at the time.

The thunderstorms began—brief showers of intense rain, with lightning and thunder, which did nothing to disturb the pall of stale heat that clung to the stinking city. They ended as suddenly as they began, and left the streets still steaming and fetid. It occurred to me that I should more actively prompt Harry to reminisce. I wondered if, between us, we might not produce a memoir of the Twenties? We would call it *An Old Man Remembers the Jazz Age,* or something of the sort; lavishly illustrated with photographs from the period, it would stand as an expressive personal document of modern America in the innocent exuberance of its golden youth. The more I thought about it, the surer I felt that such a book was needed. I mentioned the idea to Harry when next I saw him. "I knew an angel once," he murmured. "That was in the Twenties."

IT WAS, THEY SAID, THE HOTTEST SUMMER IN THIRTY years, and there was a distinct possibility that the garbage men would go on strike. A rather grisly murder occurred in an abandoned building over on Avenue C; the body was mutilated and drained of all its blood. The *New York Post* suggested that a vampire was on the loose. My own habits became increasingly nocturnal, and my productivity declined still further. I did manage to spend one afternoon in the public library looking at material from the Twenties, and made up a

6

list of questions to put to Harry, questions which I hoped would release a rich flow of anecdotes. I felt like a prospector: if only, I thought, I could sink my probe with enough precision, up would gush the stuff to make us both some real money. The times were right, I became more certain than ever, for *An Old Man Remembers the Jazz Age*.

But Harry was harder to draw out than I'd anticipated. When next I broached the topic—it was a Friday evening, and the sunset was gorgeous—he spoke again of his angel. He was relaxed and affable, I remember, and I humored him. "You mean metaphorically he was an angel, Harry," I said. "You mean he was a very good man."

"Oh, no," said Harry, turning toward me. "No, he was not a good man at all!" The armchairs were, as usual, facing the windows, angled only slightly toward each other, so we sat as if piloting some great craft into the darkling sky. "But he was a real angel, absolutely authentic."

"Who was he, Harry?"

"His name," said Harry, "was Anson Havershaw." He sat forward and peered at me. "You do want to hear the story?" he said. "I should hate to bore you."

WHEN WAS IT, PRECISELY, THAT I BEGAN TO TAKE Harry's angel seriously? I suppose there was something in the tale that caught my imagination immediately. He described to me how, as a very young man, and fresh from Harvard, he had glimpsed across the floor of an elegant New York speakeasy a man who bore a striking resemblance to himself. "An uncanny physical likeness," said Harry. "Perfectly extraordinary." He had lost sight of the man, and spent an hour looking for him, without success. He returned to the speakeasy night after night; a week later he saw him again. He introduced himself. The other was Anson Havershaw, a wealthy and sophisticated young dandy, "a much more polished character than I," said Harry, "and he recognized the similarity between us at once; it amused him. He asked me to lunch with him the following day at the Biltmore, and said that we should become friends."

All light had faded from the sky by this point. There was a long pause. "Well, we did become friends," said Harry at last, "very good friends indeed. Oh, enough, Bernard!" He was sitting with one long leg crossed over the other, ankles sockless, his left hand clutching his right shoulder and his gaze fixed on the distant spire, which glittered in the darkness like a dagger. All the tension, all the vitality seemed suddenly to drain out of him. He sat there deflated and exhausted. The room was by this time full of shadows, and Harry was slumped in his armchair like a corpse. The exertion involved in his flight of memory seemed to have sharpened the foul smell that clung to him, for the perfume could no longer mask it at all. I moved quietly to the door. "Call me," I said, "when you want to continue." A hand flapped wearily from the arm of the chair. I left him there, alone in the shadows.

"IT WAS SOME WEEKS LATER WHEN WE WERE ON TERMS OF intimacy," said Harry, when next we met, "that Anson first invited me to his house. The front door was opened by his valet, an Englishman called Allardice. He showed me into Anson's dressing room and left me there.

"I settled myself to wait. After a few minutes Anson entered in a silk dressing gown of Chinese design, followed by Allardice. He greeted me warmly and asked if Allardice could get me anything; then he told me to talk to him while he dressed—or rather, while Allardice dressed him."

A long pause here; Harry's fingers were kneading the arm of the chair. Then he began to speak quickly and warmly. "Anson stepped up to the glass and slipped the gown from his shoulders; he stood there quite naked, with one foot advanced and turned very slightly outwards, and his fingers caught lightly on his hips. How tall and slender, and hairless he was! And white, Bernard, white as milk!"

Harry at this point sat up quite erect in his armchair and lifted a hand to sketch Anson's figure in the air before him. "He had a neck like the stem of a flower," he said softly, "and narrow shoulders; and his chest was very flat, and very finely nippled, and merged imperceptibly into a belly punctuated by the merest suggestion of a navel. He stood before the glass and gazed at himself with all the impersonal admiration he might have expended on a piece of fine porcelain or a Ming vase, as though he knew he was quite beautiful, and suffered no impulse to humility on the point. . . ."

Harry turned to me and held out his glass. There were pearls of perspiration on his forehead, and his smell was very bad. I gave him more gin. "Then," he went on, "he had me come close and examine his body. There was a slight flap of skin midway between his hipbones, and believe me, Bernard, a flap is all it was; there was no knot to it. It was"—Harry groped for words—"vestigial! It was . . . decorative!"

Silence in that gloom-laden and incense-reeking room.

"I asked him what he was. 'I have not your nature,' he said quite simply. 'I am of the angels.' "

Harry's gaze shifted back to the open window. "The dressing proceeded," he whispered, "and when Anson looked upon his final perfection, Allardice came forward with a flower for his buttonhole—an orchid, I think it was; and then at last the hush and reverence were banished. 'Come, Harry,' he cried, and together we glided down the stairs, with Allardice, close behind, intent upon the flurry of instructions Anson was giving him with regard to the evening. I was, I suppose, utterly mystified, and utterly intoxicated by this time, for I followed him; I followed him like a shadow. . . ."

Harry fell silent again. His hand was still lifted in the air, and trembling, as he stared out of the window. As for myself, I felt suddenly impatient of this talk. These, I said to myself, are nothing but the gin-fired fantasies of a maudlin old queen. I muttered some excuse and left; Harry barely noticed.

THERE COMES A DAY, IN THE RIPE MATURITY OF LATE summer, when you first detect a suggestion of the season to come; often as subtle as a play of evening light against familiar bricks, or the drift of a few brown leaves descending, it signals imminent release from savage heat and intemperate growth. You anticipate cool, misty days, and a slow, comely decadence in the order of the natural. Such a day now dawned; and my pale northern soul, in its pale northern breast, quietly exulted as the earth slowly turned its face from the sun. This quickening of the spirit was accompanied, in my relationship with Harry, by disillusion and withdrawal. Oddly enough, though, I spoke of his angel to no one; it was as though I'd tucked it into some dark grotto of my brain, there to hold it secret and inviolate.

The murder victim of Avenue C, ran the prevailing theory, was a double-crosser involved in a major drug deal. The nastiness was presumed to be a warning to others not to make the same mistake. The garbage men went out on strike for three days, but a settlement was reached before things really began to go bad, and the trucks were soon rolling again—stinking ripely and clouded with insects, noxious monsters trumpeting and wheezing through the midnight streets. The one that serviced my block was called *The Pioneer*, and on the side of it was painted a covered wagon rumbling across some western prairie. When I found myself downwind of *The Pioneer*, I thought, unkindly, of Harry.

It was at around this time that I began to toy with the notion of a historical novel about heretics. I'd chanced upon a gnostic tale in which Satan, a great god, creates a human body and persuades a spirit called Arbal-Jesus to project his being into it for a few moments. Arbal-Jesus complies with Satan's seemingly innocent request, but once inside the body he finds himself trapped, and cannot escape. He screams in agony, but Satan only laughs; and then mocks his captive by sexually violating him. Arbal-Jesus' only consolation is that another spirit accompanies him in the body, and guarantees his release. That spirit is Death.

But then the brief taste of fall vanished, and the heat returned with greater ferocity than ever. On my way out one morning I met Harry. "Bernard," he said, "why do I never see you now?" I felt guilty. He looked rather more seedy than usual; his jaw was stubbled with fine white hairs, and traces of dried blood adhered to his nostrils. His bony fingers clutched my arm. "Come down this evening," he said. "I have gin." Poor old man, I thought, lonely and shabby, scraping about in two rooms after all these years . . . why does he still cling to the raft?

I knocked on Harry's door around seven. All was as usual—the smells, the gin, the Chrysler Building rising like a jeweled spearhead against the sky, and upon Harry's wall the crucifix shining in the shadows of the fading day. Poor old Harry; I sensed immediately he wanted to continue with his story, but was holding back out of deference to me. I felt compelled to re-open the subject, though not simply out of courtesy to an old man's obsession. I had been thinking some more about this shadowy figure, the beautiful, decadent Anson Havershaw, he of the milk-white flesh and the nonexistent navel, and about Harry's cryptic but no doubt carnal relationship with him. It was, I felt, a most bizarre fiction he had begun to weave about a man who, I presumed, had in fact actually existed, and indeed might still be alive.

So Harry began to talk. He described how Anson swept him into a summer of hectic and dazzling pleasures, of long nights, riotous and frenzied, when all of America seemed to be convulsed in a spasm of fevered

gaiety, and the two of the [...]
revels like a pair of gods, lang[...]
presiding with heavy-lidded eyes over [...]
That summer, the summer of 1925, Harr[...]
himself leaving Anson's house in the first [...]
dawn, still in evening clothes, and slipping into [...]
welcome gloom of St. Ignatius Loyola on Park Avenue. "You wouldn't know it, Bernard," he said; "they
tore it down in 1947. A lovely church, Gothic Revival;
I miss it . . . at the early Mass it would be lit only by
the dim, blood-red glow from the stained-glass windows, and by a pair of white candles that rose from
gilded holders on either side of the altar and threw out
a gorgeous, shimmering halo. . . . The priest I knew
well, an ascetic young Jesuit; I remember how his pale
face caught the candlelight as he turned to the congre-
gation—the whole effect was so strangely beautiful,
Bernard, if you had seen it you would understand the
attraction Catholicism held for so many of us . . . it
was the emotional appeal, really; disciplined Christi-
anity we found more difficult to embrace. . . ."

Harry rambled on in this vein for some minutes, his
eyes on the spire and his fingers curled about his glass.
My own thoughts drifted off down parallel tracks,
lulled comfortably by his voice. As a raconteur Harry
was slow and fastidious; he composed his sentences
with scrupulous care and lingered indulgently over his
more graceful phrases. "I doubt I would have done
well in business," he was saying, inconsequentially; "I
just haven't the kidney for it. One needs strong nerves,
and I was always much too effete. Anson used to say
that the world was a brothel, and he was right, of
course. So where is one to turn? I can tell you where I

...hurch!" He
...at's another
...d to be digress-
...ong ago, you see,
...n which things oc-

...rnard, that have to be
...oncerns his origins; the

AT THESE WOR... ...AN TO PAY ACTIVE ATTENTION
once more. This ang... ...usiness was, of course, nonsense;
but I had come to suspect that something rather fantastic, or even perverse, might lie behind it.

"About his origins I could learn almost nothing,"
Harry continued. "People said he arrived in New York
during the last year of the first war; he had apparently
been raised in Ireland by his mother, who was from
Boston and had married into an obscure branch of the
Havershaws of Cork, an eccentric family, so they said;
but then, you see, well-born Europeans with cloudy
origins have always been drifting into New York, and
so long as their manners and their money are adequate
—particularly the latter—they're admitted to society
and no one's very bothered about where they've come
from. We are, after all, a republic."

Boston! At the mention of Boston an idea suddenly
occurred to me. Harry was old Boston, this I knew,
and I wondered whether this angel of his might be
nothing more than an elaborate sexual disguise. Anson
Havershaw, by this theory, was simply an alter ego, a
detached figment of Harry's neurotic imagination, a

14

double or other constructed as a sort of libidinal escape valve. In other words, Harry transcended his own guilty carnality by assuming at one remove the identity of an angel—this would explain the physical resemblance between the two, and the contradictory themes of hedonism and spirituality; what Catholic, after all, lapsed or otherwise, could ever believe the body was a temple in which nothing was unclean? I watched Harry smiling to himself, and his expression, in the twilight, and despite the patrician dignity of the nose, seemed suddenly silly, pathetic.

"And his purpose?" I said drily.

"Ah." The pleasure slowly ebbed from his face, and he began to make an unpleasant sucking noise with his dentures. "Who knows?" he said at last. "Who knows what an angel would be doing in a century like this one? Maybe he was just meant to be an angel for our times." There was a long pause. "Immortal spirit burned in him, you see. . . . Sin meant nothing to him; he was pure soul. This was his tragedy."

"His tragedy?"

Harry nodded. "To be pure soul in an age that would not believe its existence." He asked me to give him more gin. I was feeling very irritable as I poured his gin.

WE SAT THERE, HARRY AND I, IN SILENCE, HE NO doubt contemplating these spurious memories of his, while I wondered how soon I could decently escape. Harry had taken from his pocket a small jade compact and was powdering his face with rapid, jerky movements, his eyes averted from me so I had only the beaky profile. "Pure soul," he repeated, in a murmur, "in an age that would not believe its existence."

"What happened to him?" I said wearily.

"Oh," he replied, snapping shut the compact, "I lost sight of him. I believe he came to a bad end; I believe he was sent to prison."

"No he wasn't."

Harry looked at me sharply. There was, for the first time in our relationship, a genuinely honest contact between us. All the rest had been indulgence on his part and acquiescence on mine. "Am I so transparent?" he said. "I suppose I must be. Dear Bernard, you're angry with me."

I rose to my feet and moved to the window and stared into the night. "I don't think Anson Havershaw ever existed," I said. "There was instead a man consumed with guilt who created a fairy story about angels and spirits in order to conceal certain truths from himself." Why, I thought, do old drunks always choose me to tell their stories to?

"I haven't told you the complete truth," said Harry.

"There was no Anson Havershaw," I said.

"Oh there was, there was. There is," said Harry. A pause. Then: "There was no Harry Talboys."

I turned. This I was not prepared for.

"I am Anson Havershaw."

I laughed.

He nodded. "I shall show you," he said, and rising to his feet, he began laboriously to remove his jacket, and then to unbutton his shirt.

*   *   *

16

IN THE MIDDLE OF HARRY'S CEILING WAS A FIXTURE INTO which three light bulbs were screwed. A short length of chain hung from it; Harry pulled the chain, and the room was flooded with a harsh raw light. Beneath his shirt, it now became apparent, he wore a garment of some sort of off-white surgical plastic. Slowly he removed his shirt. The plastic, which was quite grubby, encased him like a sleeveless tunic from his upper chest to a line somewhere below the belt of his trousers. It was fastened down the side by a series of little buckles, and a very narrow fringe of dirty gauze peeped from the upper edge, where the skin was rubbed to an angry rash. Harry's arms were the arms of a very old man, the flesh hanging from the bone in loose white withered flaps. He smiled slightly, for I suppose I must have been gazing with horrified curiosity at this bizarre corset of his. I was standing close to the incense, and as Harry fumbled with the buckles I brought the censer up under my nose; for the smell rapidly became very bad indeed. He dropped his trousers and underpants. The corset extended to his lower belly, forming a line just above a hairless pubis and a tiny, uncircumcised penis all puckered up and wrinkled in upon itself. He loosed the final straps; holding the corset to his body with his fingers, he told me gently that I must not be shocked. And then he revealed himself to me.

There was, first of all, the smell; a wave of unspeakable foulness was released with the removal of the corset, and to defend my senses I was forced to clamp my nostrils and inhale the incense with my mouth. Harry's flesh had rotted off his lower ribs and belly, and the clotted skin still clinging to the ribs and hipbones that bordered the hole was in a state of gelati-

17

nous putrescence. In the hole I caught the faint gleam of his spine, and amid an indistinct bundle of piping the forms of shadowy organs. I saw sutures on his intestines, and the marks of neat stitching, and a cluster of discolored organic vessels bound with a thin strip of translucent plastic. He should have been dead, and I suppose I must have whispered as much, for I heard him say that he could not die. How long I stood there gazing into his decaying torso I do not know; at some point I seemed to become detached from my own body and saw as if from high up and far away the two figures standing in the room, the flowers and the crucifix between them, myself clutching the censer and Harry standing with his opened body and his trousers at his ankles. It took long enough, I suppose, for the full horror of his condition to be borne home to me. This is what it means to be an angel, I remember thinking, in our times at least: eternal life burned in him while his body, his temple, crumbled about the flame. Out there in the hot night the city trembled with a febrile life of its own, and somewhere a siren leaped into sudden desolate pain. All I saw then was a young man standing in the corner of a shabby room watching an old man pull up his trousers.

As I write this it is late January, and very cold outside. Snow lies heaped in filthy piles along the edge of the sidewalk, and the Chrysler Building is a bleak gray needle against a thickening winter afternoon sky. The men from the men's shelter huddle in the doorways in the Bowery, selling cigarettes from off the tops of plastic milk crates, and the smell of incense still pervades the lower floors of the building. I can't help thinking of him as Harry—it seems somehow to suit him better. He asked me to write an account of our friendship, I wouldn't otherwise have done it; writing seems futile now. Everything seems futile, for some reason I don't fully understand, and I keep wondering why any of us cling to the raft. The one consolation I can find is the presence of that other spirit traveling with us in the body—a consolation denied my rotting friend downstairs, whoever, whatever, he is.

The Lost Explorer

ONE FRESH AND GUSTY DAY IN THE DAMP AUTUMN OF her twelfth year Evelyn found a lost explorer in the garden of her parents' London home. He was lying in a small tent beneath a mosquito net so torn and gaping as to be quite inadequate, were there any mosquitoes for it to protect him from. His clothes were stained with sweat and blood, and a grizzled beard stubbled his emaciated face. On the folding stool beside the camp bed stood a flask, empty, a revolver, unloaded, two bullets, three matches, a small oil lamp, and a dirty, creased map of the upper reaches of the Congo. He was delirious with fever and occasionally gibbered about the pygmies. Evelyn thought he was wonderful.

And he thought she was wonderful, too. When the delirium had passed and he lay, pale, spent, and shivering, she loomed out of the fog that was his consciousness like a bright ministering angel.

"Agatha," he whispered. "I want a drink of water." The angel vanished, and the explorer lay panting feebly in his tiny tent. In the deep, still place at the center of his frenzied mind a flame of hope was lit, for Agatha was here. What had happened was this: the explorer had mistaken Evelyn for the nanny who'd nursed him through a childhood illness!

Evelyn returned to the tent with a cup of water. She folded back the ragged netting and helped the explorer onto an elbow. Much of the water spilled onto his bush jacket, but at length his parched lips smacked up their fill and he lay back, exhausted. Evelyn gazed down at him with benevolent compassion.

"Agatha," he whispered, "give me your hand." She knelt on the ground beside the camp bed and took the explorer's clammy palm in her fingers. A ghost of a smile hovered at the cracked edges of the man's lips. "Agatha," he sighed; but then, seized suddenly with a fresh wave of panic, he started up from his bed. "The pygmies, Agatha!" he shouted. "I hear the pygmies!"

Evelyn remained calm. She laid her cool hand upon his fevered temples. The traffic of London murmured in the thoroughfares beyond. "They're miles away," she whispered. "They don't know you're here."

"They're coming!" he shouted, his head jerking from side to side and his red-rimmed eyes abulge. "They're coming to eat us!"

"Nonsense," breathed Evelyn, stroking that troubled brow. "No one's going to eat us."

The panic passed; a moment later the tension was visibly draining from the explorer's body. He sank back onto the camp bed. "Agatha," he said weakly, his hand still clutching hers. "You're good."

"Rest," murmured Evelyn. "Sleep. You're safe now. Sleep."

WHEN SHE WAS SURE THE EXPLORER WAS SOUND ASLEEP, Evelyn skipped up the garden to the house. A washing line was strung from a post at the top of the steps to a tree by the wall at the side of the house. To this line were pegged three white sheets, all flapping wildly in the wind. Dead leaves spun about the girl as she pattered gracefully up the steps from the garden. She opened the back door. Her mother and Mrs. Guppy were bent over the oven with their backsides to her.

"Are you quite sure it's done, Mrs. Guppy?" her mother was saying.

"It's had twenty-five minutes, Mrs. Piker-Smith. It must be done."

"Oh, I do hope so. Gerald is so fussy about his chop. Ah, there you are, Evelyn. Run and wash your hands, dear, and we'll eat."

Mrs. Piker-Smith was a plump, tweedy woman, and she was commonly in the throes of mild anxiety. Ten minutes later she sat at the dining-room table gazing at her husband, Gerald, the eminent surgeon. He in turn was gazing at his chop. Evelyn had already started to eat, and paid no attention to either of them.

"Is it all right, dear?" said Mrs. Piker-Smith. "We gave it almost half-an-hour." Her own knife and fork were poised at a shallow angle above her plate. A sudden gust rattled the windowpane. The surgeon tentatively sliced a small section of meat and raised the fork to his lips. He chewed the meat thoughtfully, his eyes wandering about the ceiling and upper walls as he did so. Finally he swallowed and, laying down his cutlery, dabbed at his lips with a starched white napkin. "It's quite thoroughly cooked, Denise," he said, his eyes suddenly settling upon his wife's troubled face. "You need not worry so."

"Oh, good," said Mrs. Piker-Smith, brightening, and with some gusto cut a potato in two. "What have you been doing all morning, Evelyn?" she said, turning to her daughter.

"Oh, nothing."

"Nothing?" said her father, eating.

"Just playing in the garden, Daddy."

"What ever does the child get up to?" he murmured, as he transferred a spot of English mustard from the side of his plate to a neat rectangle of chop.

"Daddy."

"Yes, Evelyn?"

"Are there still pygmies in the Congo?"

A frown briefly ruffled the calm surface of the surgeon's fine-domed brow, like a breeze whispering across a lake. "I believe so. Why do you ask?"

"Oh, school."

"Are you doing Africa, darling?" said Mrs. Piker-Smith.

"Sort of."

"It's not called the Congo anymore," said Daddy. "It became Zaïre when the Belgians left."

"When was that, Daddy?"

"Nineteen-sixty, I think."

*   *   *

After lunch Evelyn always had to go to her room and read on her bed for an hour. Today she stood at the bedroom window, gazing into the garden and thinking about her explorer. White clouds fled like driven rags across the blustering blue sky, and the branches of the great elm at the bottom of the garden flailed about like the arms of drowning men. The Piker-Smiths' was one of those long narrow gardens enclosed by an old wall whose crumbling red bricks were overgrown with ivy. The path ran from the foot of the back-door steps between two flowerbeds and then twisted over a stretch of lawn before arriving at a small round goldfish pond, the surface of which was half-hidden by clusters of green-fronded water lilies. Beyond the pond a gardening shed, its windows misted with dust and cobwebs and its door secured by a huge rusting padlock, clung in ramshackle fashion to the corner formed by the east wall and the end wall. The rest of the garden beyond the pond was a tangled and overgrown mass of rhododendron bushes, into whose labyrinthine depths, since the death of the old gardener, only Evelyn now ventured. It was in that tangled thicket of evergreens that the explorer's tent was pitched, and there that the man himself lay struggling with a furious malaria. The three white sheets billowed in the wind, and for an instant Evelyn imagined the house and the garden as a great ship shouldering on to the tropics. Absently she picked up a jar containing a pickled thumb that Daddy had given her. She swirled it round in its liquid and willed the time to pass.

*   *   *

WHEN HER HOUR WAS UP, EVELYN CAME DOWNSTAIRS TO find Daddy in the hall just leaving for the hospital. He was telling Mummy something about dinner: the Cleghorns were coming and there was no sherry in the house. Then Daddy said goodbye and left.

"Now, darling," said Mrs. Piker-Smith, "I'm off to my bridge. You'll be all right till Mrs. Guppy gets back?"

"Yes, Mummy."

Then Mrs. Piker-Smith left too. Evelyn was alone. She was down the back-door steps in a flash, under the billowing sheets, across the lawn and into the bushes. The explorer was still fast asleep. Evelyn knelt beside him and watched his face with intense concentration for some minutes. Then her gaze drifted to the objects on his camp stool, and settled on the black revolver. She had never touched a gun before, and it fascinated her. She reached out hesitantly, and clasped it by the grip. How cold and slippery it was! And how heavy! She lifted it and pressed the barrel to her cheek. It smelled metallic and oily. She touched it once with her tongue, and recoiled with a small shock as she tasted its steely sweetness. Ugh! She cradled it in her palms, in her lap, and stared at it solemnly. How would you put bullets into it? She could turn the cylinder, but she could not release it. Perhaps this little catch . . .

Evelyn screamed: a large, scarred hand, dark brown, very dirty, with hair on the back and cracked fingernails, had clamped onto her own slim fingers and held them fast. It was the explorer's hand. He was up on one elbow, staring at her, and his harrowed face was clenched and twitching with anger. She gazed at him with wide, shocked eyes. He took the revolver from her. "And the bullet," he growled, picking it from her open palm. He took the other bullet from the camp stool and then, his eyes darting from the girl to the revolver, he loaded two chambers.

"One for you, Agatha," he said hoarsely, "one for me." He nodded several times. "This way: quick—sure—painless. Better death, foil the pygmies, what." He subsided onto his back, suddenly exhausted. His fingers twitched upon the sweat-stained canvas of the cot, and a sudden access of perspiration left him pale and dripping. His eyes bulged, then fixed upon a point on the roof of the tent. His whole body shivered, and a limp hand fluttered from the canvas like an injured bird. "Agatha," he moaned; and Evelyn, dropping to her knees, took his hand.

ALL AFTERNOON THE FEVER RAGED, AND THE EXPLORER mumbled incoherently throughout. On several occasions he was convulsed with terror, and rose up shouting that the pygmies were hard by; but each time Evelyn calmed and soothed the troubled man, mopped his brow and gave him water; and in his few moments of lucidity he gazed at her with weak, shining eyes and murmured the name Agatha. For in the turmoil of his disordered mind he lay in a child's bedroom, in a child's bed, with a stuffed golliwog beside him, and a kindly woman in a sort of ruffled white cap and a starched white apron briskly ministering to his child's disease; and thus did Evelyn appear to him.

When the light began at last to thicken, and the dusk of that autumnal day crept into the explorer's tent and pooled itself in clots of shadow in the corners of the tent, a voice came calling, "Evelyn! Evelyn!" The man stirred in his uneasy doze, muttering, and Evelyn leaned close to him. "I have to go," she whispered. "Sleep now, and I'll come back. . . ."

He seemed about to rise from the camp bed and cry out; his eyes opened wide for an instant; but then the netherworld of shadows and confusion reclaimed him, and he sank once more into sleep of a sort. Evelyn spread upon his twitching limbs the blanket she had brought out from the house; and then she padded silently away, through the bushes, and onto the path back to the house.

THE CLEGHORNS WERE OLD FRIENDS OF THE FAMILY, SO Evelyn was permitted to eat with the grown-ups. Mrs. Cleghorn—Auntie Vera—was a large dark woman with good teeth. She wore heavy lipstick and was married to an anesthetist called Frank—Uncle Frank—a colleague of Gerald's. Mummy and Auntie Vera often played bridge together, and it was about bridge that they were talking when Evelyn entered the drawing room, just before dinner. Everybody was drinking a rather nice South African sherry, and Evelyn was invited to have a juice. Then Mrs. Piker-Smith went to see Mrs. Guppy in the kitchen, and as the two men drew aside to talk shop for a moment Auntie Vera's great black eyes swiveled round on Evelyn like a pair of undimmed headlights.

"Evelyn," she cried, plumping a cushion with a large white hand. "Come here and sit next to me. How is school?" Evelyn liked Auntie Vera, but she

27

was rather in awe of her. She sat down on the sofa, pressing her slender legs together and clasping her hands in her lap. "We're on half-term," she said, looking at the carpet.

"Half-term!" cried Auntie Vera. "How marvelous!"

"Yes," said Evelyn with great seriousness. "Do you know anything about Africa, Auntie Vera?" A coal fire crackled in the grate; above the mantelpiece hung a mirror, and invitations to social functions, mostly connected to the hospital, were tucked into the inside edge of the frame.

"Frank took me to Cairo for our honeymoon," said Auntie Vera, taking Evelyn's hand. "He pretended I was Cleopatra!" Evelyn turned toward her and found the great black headlamps shining with delight and the tip of Auntie Vera's tongue resting on her top lip.

Conversation at the dinner table ranged widely from the price of sherry to the price of beef. Gerald mentioned a rather interesting colostomy he'd performed after lunch, and Uncle Frank made some quips which might, in a nonmedical household, have been taken in rather bad taste. Only once did Evelyn pay any attention, and that was during the main course, when Auntie Vera turned to her husband and said, "Frank, Evelyn is interested in Africa."

"*Is* she?" said Frank Cleghorn.

"Not all Africa, Uncle Frank," said Evelyn. "Just the Congo."

"Ah, the Congo!" said Uncle Frank fatly, and began to tell the story of Henry Morton Stanley, digressing rather amusingly to mention the tragic shooting death of John Hanning Speke mere hours before the eagerly awaited debate with Richard Burton on the source of the Nile; that was in 1864. Evelyn was sitting opposite Uncle Frank, who had his back to the door of the dining room, which was half-open; as Evelyn half-listened to his affable drone, she suddenly saw, over his shoulder, pausing in the doorway as he shuffled towards the stairs, the explorer. He turned his head and stared at her. Fortunately, she did not cry out; Auntie Vera was deep in animated bridge talk with Mummy, and Daddy was concentrating on a delicate incision he was about to make in a slice of reddish beef. Uncle Frank warbled on, and in the doorway behind his back stood the haggard, feverish man, and oh, how ill he looked! His head hung weakly on sagging shoulders; his eyes burned with a low, sickly gleam out of sunken sockets in an unshaven face deeply etched with gullies of suffering. His clothes looked extraordinarily ragged and filthy against the beige flowered wallpaper of the hallway, and his scarred, grimy hands still twitched convulsively where they dangled at his sides. Evelyn stared at him wide-eyed, and Uncle Frank was flattered at the raptness of her attention. It was only after some moments that he realized her eyes were focused not upon his own but beyond them; and he began, even as his discourse flowed forward, to turn in his seat. But at precisely the same instant the explorer shuffled off down the hallway out of sight; so that Uncle Frank, seeing nothing, turned back and talked on. Daddy, having completed his incision, lifted his fork and his eyes and turned to the anesthetist as his teeth closed upon the meat; and Auntie Vera lifted her wineglass while Mummy peered anxiously into the gravy boat.

When at last Evelyn was able to get away, she

dashed upstairs; and as she had half-feared, and half-hoped, the explorer was in her bedroom. Not only was he in her bedroom, he was in her *bed,* fully clothed, the sheets up to his chin. His teeth were chattering loudly and his whole body shivered beneath the bedclothes.

"Cold," he grunted as Evelyn closed the door behind her and ran to the bed. "Cold, Agatha," he said more clearly, and she reached under the bedclothes for his hand. It was frigid. Something else was down there too—she felt the hard metallic bulge of the revolver, stuffed into the explorer's waistband. "Let me have the gun," she whispered.

A tremor passed across the pathetic features of the dying man. "Need will," he muttered. "Need will to do it. Pygmies . . ." Here he paused, and his chest heaved painfully with the effort to talk, the effort to think. Oh, how he wanted simply to slip away, let go, sink into peace and rest and silence and darkness! —but he could not let go, not yet. "Pygmies," he said, more loudly, and Evelyn with terror clapped her hand upon his parched and cracking lips. The wild eyes darted to her bedroom door. He knew they were near. "Pygmies," he whispered, when she lifted her palm from his mouth. "Coming to eat us. One for you, Agatha, one for me . . ."

"Don't talk," said Evelyn, her finger to her lips. "We won't be eaten. Sleep. I'll give you a drink."

Evelyn fetched a drink of water, and the explorer's eyes, as she supported his shoulders and held the cup to his lips, rested on her face with an expression of such profound pain, and gratitude, and spirit that it tested the girl's mettle pretty sternly. But she did not

30

flinch nor falter, and when he had drunk she eased his head back onto her pillow and stroked his chilly brow.

"Agatha," he murmured, "Agatha," and his grip on her fingers loosened very slightly.

THE REST OF THAT EVENING WAS NERVE-RACKING FOR Evelyn. She went downstairs to say good night to Uncle Frank and Auntie Vera, and to Mummy and Daddy, and then darted back up to her bedroom. She could only hope that Mummy wouldn't come to tuck her in tonight; it was something she did occasionally, by no means invariably. Evelyn made up a bed for herself on the carpet, and turned off the light. The explorer seemed to be sleeping soundly. She listened in the darkness for Mummy and Daddy coming up to bed. Daddy was first; she heard him brushing his teeth in the bathroom. Then Mummy came up, and stopped at the top of the stairs. Evelyn's heart was beating fit to burst; hot chemicals discharged and flooded in turmoil about her viscera; go to bed, Mummy, a voice in her brain screamed silently, *go to bed, Mummy!* Steps across the landing, and then—*a hand on Evelyn's door handle!*

The tension, in the few moments that followed, was, to Evelyn, lying there in the darkness, her eyes wide and her stomach awash with adrenaline, almost unendurable. Frightful scenarios unfolded at lightning speed in her febrile imagination. How could Mummy and Daddy be expected to understand about the explorer? And the gun! What if—

"Denise!"

Even as the handle turned, her father's voice called from the bathroom.

"What is it, Gerald?" replied her mother in hushed tones.

"Have we any dental floss?"

"On the shelf, dear." The door handle was still depressed; Evelyn desperately wanted to go to the bathroom herself.

"No, I don't see it."

"Oh, Gerald," murmured Mrs. Piker-Smith; and, wifely duty superseding maternal solicitude in the ethical hierarchy of that good woman, she tiptoed to the bathroom and located the dental floss. A short conversation about the beef ensued; and then Mrs. Piker-Smith went into the bedroom, closely followed by her husband, and their door, to Evelyn's immense relief, closed behind them. But it was another excruciating hour before she dared get up and creep to the bathroom.

THE NEXT MORNING THE EXPLORER WAS DEAD. SILENTLY, and, one hopes, peacefully, in the middle of the night, he had passed away. Evelyn awoke at six and realized it immediately. He was stiff and staring, and when she laid her hand upon his face, his skin was even colder than it had been last night. She closed his eyes; and then she lay on the bed beside him, on top of the blankets, and she wept quietly for ten minutes. She wept into her blankets as the fact of the loss of that long-suffering man rose up starkly in her heart, and she wept too for herself, for she was desolate. Her sorrow was keen, but it would not fester; and when she rose from her bed, wet-eyed and gulping back the hot taste of grief in her throat, she tried to think clearly what was best. But first she must air the room, and the bed, and change the sheets, for the stink of a man too long in the jungle hung heavy in Evelyn's bedroom.

Fever had weakened him, diminished him, and the body was light. Evelyn, though skinny, was strong from hockey, and she dragged him from the bed to the closet quite easily. She sat him in the darkest corner, covered him up with a pair of old school raincoats, and pushed all her clothes to that end of the rail. Then she opened wide the windows, stuffed the sheets into her laundry basket, and climbed under the blankets, where she lay in a state of rising anxiety till Mummy should come to wake her.

"Darling, you'll catch your death!" cried Mrs. Piker-Smith when she came in at half past eight. The windows were wide open and the day was very blustery indeed. The curtains flapped wildly and the air was chill. Even so, there were traces. "What's that funny smell, darling?" said Mummy, standing by the closet door and wrinkling her nose. Evelyn, simulating a slow awakening, mumbled incomprehensibly from the bed. Mrs. Piker-Smith stood frowning a moment more. "It must be your hockey things," she decided. "Give them to Mrs. Guppy, darling, and they'll be clean for school."

Mumble.

"It's eight-thirty, darling"—and she went downstairs.

EVELYN STOOD PANTING IN THE TENT. ALL MORNING THE explorer had remained in her closet, and those hours had not been easy for the girl. But after lunch Daddy had gone back to the hospital, Mummy had gone to her bridge, and Mrs. Guppy had gone shopping. Evelyn breathed a prayer of thanks that all their lives were subject to such seemingly immutable routine. She'd hauled him out of the closet then and dragged him downstairs. She'd moved slowly, backwards, clutching him by the armpits. His head lolled about on his chest and his feet bumped limply on the stairs. In death he seemed so small, so light, that Evelyn was again unhappy, and her eyes brimmed with tears as she dragged him across the linoleum of the kitchen floor. She laid him down for a moment and went for a glass of water. Over the sink was the kitchen window, and it looked down on the garden. Mrs. Guppy had brought in the three white sheets; her own sheets had not yet replaced them; instead, the line was alive in the wind with her parents' underwear. The elm at the bottom of the garden was once more whipping its limbs about. A large Persian cat paused upon the wall by the gardener's old shed, then stalked off with dignity, picking a path along the top of the wall with its tail stiffly aloft. Evelyn had drunk her water and then manhandled the explorer down the steps, between the flowerbeds, across the lawn and round the goldfish pond, into the bushes and so to the tent. And now she would bury him.

Evelyn had long since broken open the old padlock on the shed door, and it hung there now only to hold the door. She slipped it out of the eye and the door swung open. A damp, fetid smell, dusty, earthy, filled the shed. The light with difficulty penetrated the place; a large heap of sacks moldered gently in the corner, and the old plank floor was suspiciously damp thereabouts. Evelyn had once poked about in that corner, but now she tended to avoid it, for the floor was rotten beneath the sacks, and the three substances, sacking, wood, and the earth beneath the rotten wood, had begun to coalesce, as if attempting, in their nostalgia for some primeval state of slime, to abandon structure and identity, all that could distinguish or separate them. Other signs of regression and breakdown were manifest in that dusty old shed; upon the windowsill, beneath the vast network of cobwebs, lay the stiff little corpses, some partially digested, of flies and other small winged insects, many with their tiny legs curled pathetically over them as if in a final and futile gesture of self-closure. An old cardboard box, moist with decay, was damply merging with the wall, and in it a heap of parts from some long-forgotten automobile engine congealed blackly rigid, petrifying like coal as the work of time and damp smudged them with rust and rendered their decadent inutility ever more irrevocable. Photographs had once been pinned to the wall of the shed; these now curled at the edges like the legs of the flies, and as regards their degenerated content barely a trace could now be detected of the humans who had stood, once, before the camera, vital, one presumes, and alive. It was as though they had died in the bad air, the malaria, of that neglected little corner of the garden, the thin dusty air of the old shed, within which everything must devolve to a fused state of formless unity. . . .

But Evelyn had no time to relish regression today. She stepped across the floor and seized up a spade, its blade spotted orange with rust but its handle as yet sturdy and whole. This she took from the shed and, closing the rickety door behind her and replacing the great padlock, ran back through the windy sunshine of that October afternoon and again entered the bushes.

And now she worked briskly and methodically. She collapsed the filthy tent, noticing as she did so the multitudes of tiny equatorial insects clustering in the seams and corners. She dropped it in the corner of the clearing, and then laid the explorer upon it, and his bed beside him, and then the camp stool with its few pitiful possessions—remnants of the explorer's last wild dash from the Congo, pursued by anthropophagous pygmies who had once existed either in the reality of that far jungle or in the fevered mind of her strange and needy visitor, Evelyn could not know which. And then she dug. For two hours she dug; her young limbs strong from hockey, she tore a steadily widening, steadily deepening hole out of the earth in the center of the clearing in the midst of the rhododendron bushes at the bottom of the garden. And when she was finished she lined the hole with the tent. And then she burned that old map of his, creased and sweat-stained; she set it afire with the odd vestas he had left on the folding stool, and the ashes fell into the pit. And then she tossed in the gun, having hauled it with a sob from the dead man's waistband; and then the flask and the oil lamp, and then the man himself, into his grave, but not unmourned, and maybe this is all that any of us can ask for.

SHE SAW HIM, OCCASIONALLY, IN THE MONTHS THAT followed, always from her bedroom window when the moon was up. He'd be standing at the goldfish pond, his face pale and gleaming in the moonlight and his hands twitching at his sides. He'd look up at her window and she'd slowly move her palm back and forth in greeting. And though the fever was still upon him, he seemed no longer in mortal fear of the pygmies—yes, a subtle theme of peace had entered the symphony of his diseased being, if being indeed he was. Perhaps, after all, he was nothing; Evelyn began to see him less and less frequently after that, and at around the time—she'd have been about fourteen-and-a-half then—the time she decided to become a doctor, he disappeared from her life completely, and she never saw him again.

The Black Hand of the Raj

NINETEENTH-CENTURY IMPERIALISM, AS LENIN UNDER-stood it, appeared when the great European capitalists began to have difficulty finding sound investment opportunities for their superfluous wealth at home. They turned to Africa and the East, and backed by the armed might of the state and an ideology of racial superiority proceeded to expand. Expansion bred competition, and competition bred war. War, of course, breeds only death, and death breeds nothing except maybe flowers and vegetables, which are good only for antiquated agricultural economies. What this rather gloomy analysis tends to ignore, however, is Imperialism's other face, which is indeed more properly the preserve of fiction. This is the soft face of Imperialism, and it concerns itself with human relationships, and individual psychology—and not least with the education of the senses. For it was in the torrid climates of the various far-flung corners of the Empire that many

38

Europeans first confronted the nature of passion. Frequently the experience proved liberating, and the traveler emerged from the glowing crucible a richer, wiser, and more fully rounded human being. But occasionally, the encounter of East and West, of the sensual and the rational, did not resolve so satisfactorily. Occasionally, darker forces seemed to be at work, forces committed to discord and antipathy between the races. The Black Hand of the Raj was one such force.

IT IS A WARM NIGHT IN THE SPRING OF 1897, AND GAZING at the stars from the upper deck of a P & O liner bound for Bombay stands a young woman named Lucy Hepplewhite. Her hands rest lightly upon the rough dark wood of the rail, and her face is bathed in moonlight. A soft breeze lifts the delicate tassels of the lace mantilla she has thrown about her shoulders, and gently ruffles the curls escaping from her piled tresses. Her dark eyes are misted and shining, and from between her soft lips small pearly teeth gleam like stars. But what is it that brings now a gentle smile to those ripe lips? What is she thinking of, this flower of Victorian maidenhood, as she turns her gaze to the gleaming surface of the darkly heaving waters below? She is thinking of the altar. She is thinking of love. For she is going to India to marry a young man in the Indian Civil Service to whom she became engaged some six months previously. His name is Cecil Pym, and he occupies an important post in Poonah. It is there that the happy couple will be married, and afterwards honeymoon elsewhere in the hill country. The prospect arouses in Lucy a strange excitement, a vague and delicious warmth that she is hesitant to define; then the sea breeze freshens and she turns, with a last glance at the moonlit swells, and goes below, leaving the deck deserted.

THE VOYAGE WAS UNEVENTFUL FOR THE MOST PART, AND Lucy amused herself with a little bridge, an occasional game of deck quoits, and pleasant expectations of connubial bliss with Cecil. The prospect of life in India had never unduly alarmed her; however, as the great vessel slipped down the Suez Canal, the weather grew uncomfortably warm and brought an immoderate flush to her pale cheek. She retired to her cabin and was troubled, for the first time in her life, by thoughts that were less than spotlessly pure. And in that moment the first faint whisper of a doubt as to how she would cope with the weather began to disturb her serenity.

But she did not brood upon the matter, for it was not in her nature to do so. She banished the shadow that had fallen briefly across her mind, and carried a parasol whenever she promenaded. And in the fullness of time the ship docked at Bombay, and Lucy Hepplewhite made her way gingerly down the gangway and into the arms of a tall young Englishman in a high white pith helmet and a cream-colored suit of fine Madras cotton with a pale thin stripe of eggshell blue.

Only one incident marred their happy reunion, and that was a one-handed leper who emerged from the milling dockside crowd and, grinning hideously, shoved his begging bowl in Lucy's face. Cecil saw him off quickly enough, and Lucy, who was a girl of pretty stout kidney, was not unduly distraught. Still, as they trotted toward the Empress Hotel in a tonga for tea, she could detect the telltale signs of a light perspiration breaking out beneath her cotton underclothing. She was frankly relieved when they finally escaped the blazing Bombay sun and found shelter in the cool depths of the Empress.

LUCY HAD HEARD THAT MEN CHANGED AFTER BEING IN India for even a short while; and later that night, as she sat in Cecil's compartment on the train to Poonah, she asked herself if *he* had. The answer was, alas, yes. The spirited and carefree young man she'd known in England had become quiet, and rather inward. He seemed depressed. He rarely laughed, and often his eyes drifted off into the middle distance, and became clouded, as if with some private anguish. Whatever that anguish was, Lucy was resolved that once in Poonah, and the wedding behind them, she would soothe it with womanly balm and restore him to a state of untroubled happiness. And then another question popped into her mind.

"Cecil?"

"Darling?" He turned to her from the window, whence he had been gazing with a frown of perplexity into the hot living night of India.

"Why do you never take off your pith helmet?"

It was true. Ever since he'd met her at the docks the pith helmet had not once been doffed. Not that it didn't add a certain commanding elegance to his appearance—but the question seemed to disturb him. His jaw tightened and the finely chiseled nostrils quivered slightly.

"Must I?" he murmured. "Now?"

And then, to Lucy's amazement, he pounded the door of the compartment with his fist and began sobbing uncontrollably!

"Darling!" she cried, gathering him into her arms. "Cecil, what is it? Is it—too tight?" And she reached for the pith helmet.

"No!" He leaped away from her, clutching his headgear to his skull.

"Cecil, you must tell me," whispered Lucy, gazing at him with distress and concern. It was a warm night, and she was beginning to feel damp again.

There was a long silence. The engine chuffed on through the darkness, and the rails chattered beneath them. Far off in the hills a wild dog began howling at the moon. Cecil was hunched forward in his seat, his elbows on his knees and his head in his hands. And then he turned toward her, and she saw that his face was haggard with pain.

"Very well," he said quietly, "I'll tell you."

IT WAS NOT A LONG STORY, NOR WAS IT A HAPPY ONE. Lucy heard it through to the bitter end, defying convention by staying in Cecil's compartment through the hours of darkness. But they were, after all, soon to be married.

He first described to her a little ruined summerhouse in an overgrown garden not far from his bungalow in the British cantonment in Poonah. Long since abandoned to the monkeys and the insects, and colonized by luxuriant vines whose great drooping flowers emanated odors of incense and musk, it was yet a pleasant shady spot for a smoke after dinner, and Cecil had come to think of it as his own. And then one day he'd found a little old man with a bald head and a loincloth meditating there. He'd scrounged a cigarette from Cecil and then blessed him by laying his hands on Cecil's head. Cecil had thought nothing of it at the time, but the next day he'd felt a slight irritation where the old man had touched him, and the day after that a small brown lump had appeared on his crown. Then the lump had started to grow, and it had been growing ever since. When Cecil went to the doctor—an old boy named Cadwallader, not up to much on account of the pink gins—he'd been told to come back in a week.

"But after a week," said Cecil—and then broke down for the second time. Again Lucy took him in her arms, and murmured words of comfort. Finally the young Englishman sat up straight, and pluckily unbuckled the thin leather strap fastened snugly beneath his chin.

IN INDIA, THE APPEARANCE OF A CERTAIN SORT OF PLUMP and blustery raincloud is a sure sign that the monsoons are at hand. One such cloud drifted now across the moon and threw the swaying compartment into deep shadow. So it was that when Cecil slowly removed the pith helmet, Lucy was at first uncertain what exactly she was looking at. Her first thought was of a dark brown lily splayed limply from a short thick stem attached somehow to Cecil's skull; but how could that be? And then the raincloud drifted on and in the sudden glow of moonlight she realized that the brown

43

stem was in fact a *wrist;* that it was *growing* out of Cecil's head; and that the dark limp lily atop it was a *hand!*

For a dreadful moment all sympathy fled Lucy's heart, and she knew only horror. She stared aghast at the gruesome sprout, and her own hands flew to her mouth. Cecil watched her from hooded and anguished eyes. "Now you see why I wear my pith helmet," he said, and covered the alien extremity.

There was little left to tell. Once the hand had come through, it proved to be rather active, constantly pulling his hair and sticking its fingers in his ears. Dr. Crumbler had refused to amputate, saying it was connected to the brainstem, and instead prescribed a heavy sedative. Twice a day Cecil would have to inject a few cc. into the thing's wrist to keep it quiet. "In fact," he said, glancing at his watch, "it's about time. Darling, would you mind?"

And so, as the first pale streaks of dawn crept over the land, Lucy Hepplewhite assisted her fiancé in injecting a heavy dose of some powerful narcotic into the wrist growing out of the top of his head. It was not a pleasant task, and when it was all over she slumped into her seat, exhausted, while Cecil turned again to the window.

ONCE IN POONAH, LUCY WAS DROPPED OFF AT THE Florence Nightingale Residence for Young Women, and she kissed Cecil fondly before he went on to his own bungalow. Deep shadows had appeared around the young man's eyes, and in the light of early morning a note of gaunt and terrible despair could be detected in his features. He seemed, again, broken and helpless before his grim fate, and Lucy's heart went out to him. "Don't torment yourself, darling," she whispered, laying her small white palm on his cheek. "I'm here now."

"But how can you love a man with a hand growing out of his head?" he whispered furiously.

"Trust me," murmured Lucy; but she was never to see him alive again.

Lucy retired to her room at the residence and fell asleep almost immediately. Her dreams were less than tranquil, however; she tossed and turned beneath her mosquito net, and through the turbulent flood of images that coursed about her fevered mind, one reared up with greater frequency and intensity than all the others—and that was the hand growing out of Cecil's head. But in Lucy's dream it was not sedated—very far from it: it writhed and twisted and beckoned and pointed, it throbbed and undulated like a serpent, and performed gestures of an unspeakably lewd nature. Lucy awoke with a wild cry of panic, and the hand disappeared. But the sensation persisted, and she found she was perspiring heavily.

She arose, rather weakly, soon after, and bathed, unable to sleep more; and some hours later found her way across the cantonment to Cecil's bungalow. No servant answered the door, so she quietly let herself in. It was late afternoon now, and very still. She called Cecil's name; the sound died in the deep silence that lay upon the place like a pall, and the girl shivered. Shadows were beginning to gather in the corners of Cecil's neat and sparsely furnished sitting room. Beside a low couch upholstered in black leather a whisky bottle, a soda siphon, and a glass of cut crystal stood upon a small table. On one wall hung a sepia-toned photograph of Cecil at Oxford, and beside it her own image. She gazed at them wistfully. Would she ever see that smile of guileless charm upon the young man's face again? For a moment the dream returned, and a light flush crept over her cheeks.

"Cecil!" she called. "Cecil!"

Still nothing; so she passed through the sitting room and into the hallway beyond, at the end of which stood a closed door. That, she guessed, was his bedroom; and then a terrible feeling of nameless dread leaped up within her, and she resisted only with difficulty a fierce impulse to flee the place. Resolutely, though, she advanced, and now she thought she could hear something in the room beyond, a sort of furtive, muffled, slithering sound. A prickle of fear ran up Lucy Hepplewhite's spine, and a gust of adrenaline welled in her belly.

"Cecil!" she called again, walking unsteadily toward his bedroom.

The slithering sound had stopped, and Lucy's hand was upon the doorknob. She took a deep breath, then threw open the door—and such was the sight that met her eyes that a violent spasm seized her slight frame, and a scream died on her lips. For there on the floor by the unmade bed lay the half-naked body of Cecil Pym, his face purple, his eyes bulging, his tongue protruding grotesquely, and the heavy bruises of strangulation dark upon his sunburned neck! Beside him lay a hypodermic syringe, the plunger yet undepressed, and the third hand, still very much attached to the dead man's crown, lying palm down on the floor, the fingers slightly curled.

For some minutes Lucy stood there rigid with horror, and no sound escaped her. And then a choked sob finally burst free and she flung herself on him. "Oh, Cecil," she whimpered, clinging to his still-warm body, "who has done this thing to you?" She touched him with frantic fingers, searching for life, but there was none. How long she lay there as the shadows gathered about her and the insects began their shrill and rasping chorus in the dusk, she would never know. But suddenly she became aware that her hair was being very gently stroked.

"Cecil," she murmured. "Cecil, are you still with me?"

And in a way he was; for the dark hand growing out of his head had begun to softly caress Lucy's hair. And such was the lightness, the delicacy of its touch, that the demented girl did not recoil in horror, but remained, sobbing, on the corpse, as the hand soothed her and calmed her and brought her slowly to a state of passive languor; and when it gently touched her neck she still did not resist, did not leap back in disgust, but allowed the fingers to melt her pain to pleasure and revive the longings that had first been spawned by the hot sun of Suez; and once again Lucy Hepplewhite was filmed with perspiration, and she moaned in the shadows of the body of her lover.

When she arose from the body an hour later, her cotton underclothing was in a state of disarray and two red stains of shame burned upon her cheeks. Her hair was damply plastered to her brow, and a deep tranquility smoldered in her drowsy eyes. The hand lay still and quiet now, palm upwards, and Cecil was beginning to go bad. So without further ado Lucy

47

adjusted her dress, tidied her hair, and washed her face in a basin of cold water. And then she went to look for Dr. Cadwallader.

"BAD BUSINESS," MUTTERED THE PORTLY AND FLORID physician, standing over the body and reeking of gin. He shook his head as the servants placed Cecil's three-handed corpse onto a stretcher and covered it with a white sheet. "Black Hand of the Raj," he said, turning to Lucy, who was sniffling quietly into a lace handkerchief. "Always fatal. Couldn't tell him that, of course."

"You mean it's happened before?" said Lucy, glancing up sharply.

" 'Fraid so," said Cadwallader. "Lost a number of good men this way. Never can find the little fellow in the loincloth. Some sort of wog curse I suppose." And he put his plump fingers to his throat as if to demonstrate. It was at that precise moment that Lucy finally succumbed to stress, and fainted, and was revived only with great difficulty, a heavy dose of smelling salts, and a small glass of brandy from a bottle which the doctor happened to be carrying in his black bag.

INDIA BEING RATHER A WARM COUNTRY, IT WAS NECES-sary to bury Cecil Pym the very next day. Happily, he did not take the black hand with him to the grave: Cadwallader severed it with a surgical saw and a cou-ple of sharp knives, pickled it in vinegar, and depos-ited the jar in a cupboard with a number of other carefully labeled specimens. The funeral went off smoothly enough, as these things go. Lucy, veiled and lovely in black crêpe de chine, hung grieving on the porky arm of the doctor throughout, and the sun beat down on the small group of late-Victorian colonials with an intense and unrelenting ferocity. It was only when the minister began to pray for the deceased that she looked up, disturbed by Cadwallader's reaching to remove his hat. And as her damp eye blearily scanned the mourners at the graveside, it was with a ghastly tremor of foreboding that she counted no fewer than seven Englishmen conspicuous for not having removed their headgear— and the Deputy Commissioner was among them!

After the funeral Lucy did not linger long in Poonah, nor indeed in India. Within a week she had boarded a ship for home. The Lucy who left Bombay, however, was a very different creature from the one who had arrived there mere days before. She played no bridge now, and could not be tempted to deck quoits. Instead, she leaned on the rail, still in black, gazing out to sea. And by the time she was under an English heaven once more, she had reached her decision.

TWENTY-FIVE YEARS AGO TODAY AN OLD NUN WAS BURIED in the graveyard of a small convent in Tunbridge Wells. Her name was Mother Constance, but we know her better as Lucy Hepplewhite. Yes, she had joined the Sisters of Perpetual Atonement and lived out her days behind the cloister walls. She took no interest in the great events that rocked the subcontinent in the half-century or so after her departure. Instead, she became a model of piety and self-sacrifice, offering prayers without stint for the soul of poor dead Cecil Pym, and wondering, in her heart of hearts, what, exactly, was the nature of the sin she had committed.

Lush Triumphant

TUCKED INTO THE BODY OF AN OLD WAREHOUSE HALF-
way down a broken street in the meat district of
Manhattan is a little restaurant called Dorian's which
in the fall and winter of 1986 enjoyed a brief vogue.
On the floor above Dorian's worked the painter Jack
Fin. His was one of those barnlike lofts with a high tin
ceiling and primitive fixtures, ranks of canvases stacked
against the walls and, at the back, close by the couch
he slept on, a woodburning stove with a crooked chimney that found its way out through the bricks over-
looking the narrow alley where Dorian's garbage cans
were lined up along a fraying wire-mesh fence. Jack
Fin would stand at his front window at night, smoking,
with a Scotch in his hand, and watch the cabs discharge fashionable downtown diners who clustered chattering at the restaurant door and then vanished into
the warmth within. The irritability this spectacle aroused
in him increased in direct proportion to the amount of

Scotch he drank; and it was exacerbated by the odors
that seeped up from the kitchen and contaminated the
loft's native air, thick with turpentine and oil paint and
woodsmoke.

One night Jack Fin walked down to the Hudson.
The waterfront to the west of the meat district is a
desolate and sinister place; a rotting wharf juts into
the river, and little stirs save a furtive rat and the
ill-sprung chassis of a '67 Plymouth the owner of which
is copping a swift blowjob on the way home to Jersey.
Jack Fin liked it; sinister desolation was his painterly
métier, and he would tell you, if you asked him, that
the waterfront was never the same any two nights. He
sat down on a crag of shattered concrete and observed
moonlight spilling onto the water and, some way down
from him, a boy emerging from the Plymouth. The car
backed up and moved off toward the Holland Tunnel;
the boy smoothed the front of his pants, then picked
his way through the rubble. Far off, on the Jersey
shore, a hooter sounded. A siren moaned on Ninth
Avenue. The boy approached Jack and asked him for
a cigarette.

Jack gave him a cigarette, and as the match flared
Jack saw that he was very young, about thirteen, and
slim, his eyes lined with kohl. The face was soft, like a
girl's, lit from beneath by the glowing tip of the cigarette. Again the hooter sounded on the Jersey shore,
and the boy walked away, glancing back once.

Jack did not follow him. He rose from the concrete
and headed for home. Where Gansevoort meets Washington three manholes were spewing up thick clouds of
steam, and the narrow street, a ravine between darkened, long-porched warehouses, was filled and chok-

ing with it, like a sort of hell. Jack moved forward into this hell, breasting it like a swimmer, and for a moment the whiteness swirled about him and rendered his black-coated form indistinct, phantasmal even, before it swallowed him up. The steam continued to pour silently from beneath the street, and then a huge garbage truck with silver horns mounted on the cab came thundering through, and on its radiator in flowing golden script was painted the word MYSTIC.

HE DECIDED TO HAVE A NIGHTCAP IN DORIAN'S. IT WAS A Sunday, late, and the restaurant was empty. Once, this had been an unpretentious diner: a formica-topped counter with aluminum napkin dispensers and bottles of ketchup running the length of the west wall, seating on the right, a narrow channel between. But all that had changed. A series of Doric columns, structurally useless, set off the dining area, where, upon fluted, semicylindrical pillars placed at intervals flush to the wall, stood half-draped plaster figures in a variety of pseudoclassical poses. From the high white ceiling, vertical clusters of pastel-hued fluorescent tubes suffused the space with a glow that tinted the figures and columns to subtly decadent effect; and to see Dorian's running at capacity, the babble of chatter punctuated by whinnies of laughter and clinking glass, one suspected that this was the frenzied banquet that would witness at midnight the sudden cessation of music, the revelers' silence, and the entrance of some masked figure of mortality. So it seemed to Jack Fin, at any rate. But not this night; this night it was late, it was empty, and he eased himself onto a stool at the marbled bar and ordered a Scotch.

Jack sat with his elbows on the bar, the glass between his fingers, and stared at his reflection in the beveled glass behind the bottles. He saw the square face of a man in his mid-forties with untidy, ill-cut black hair, whisky-paunched cheeks, and a small chin berthed in the nascent swell of a thickening throat. His coat collar was turned up, and he was unshaven. He was thinking, though, not about his appearance but about his work, his painting, his single consuming passion.

JACK ROSE EARLY AND WORKED FOR AN HOUR. HE DID not use an easel; the canvas was stapled directly to the wall, and standing before it was his work trolley—a stainless steel structure which had come from the kitchen of a defunct restaurant and ran on casters. Its shelves were clogged now with jars of soaking brushes and crusted tools, tubes of paint in varying states of constriction, rags and bottles and cardboard boxes paint-smudged with fingerprints. When he pushed the trolley to one side, the jars and bottles all clinked together and the fluids sloshed about. He retired to the far side of the loft, where he sat on a hard chair and smoked a cigarette, gazing at the canvas as the sunshine of the morning settled on it in thick bright bars.

It was a night scene, a nocturne, called *Wharf*. The river was black, the wharf itself ruined and broken, a confused structure of tarred timbers lurching at drunken angles. Where everything is falling, nothing falls: Jack had attempted to translate Montaigne's words into graphic terms, such that his river and night sky offered no stable plane against which falling or sinking could occur. There was no horizon, and when the painting worked, thought Jack, there would not even be the memory of a horizon. Tarred timbers obsessed him: bitumen—mineral pitch, asphaltic residue, distilled essence of wood tar—"blacked and browned in the depths of hell." Such a painting had no place for a figure, and yet there was a figure, a ghost for the ruin, a black ghost with hooded, hanging head, gazing at the black river-sky from amid the cluttered timbers. Jack recognized the figure as the boy from the Plymouth; and rising from the chair, he hauled the trolley in front of the canvas and began to paint.

After an hour he left off to go for breakfast. The meat district was very much alive this time of the morning; in a cloud of blue exhaust fumes a truck backed up across the sidewalk, and from the opened warehouse came a blast of refrigerated air. Within, the headless carcasses of skinned hogs hung from hooks, and white-coated, misty-breathed men in bloodstained aprons unhurriedly butchered huge sides of meat. Jack skirted a large red garbage can with the word INEDIBLE stenciled on the side and containing a heap of kidneys, heads, chunks of fat, pieces of feet, and a single unblinking eyeball. The air was pungent with the smell of cold meat, and black garbage bags lay piled against the wall beside an unsteady structure of wooden boxes. Jack stepped into the street, inadvertently kicking a stray chipped liver, which skittered into a puddle and sank from sight. It was a bright day, but cold, and Jack was briskly rubbing his hands as he entered the steamed-up coffee shop where he took most of his meals. He pushed through the knot of white-coated meat packers to the counter and, settling on a stool, ordered breakfast. The coffee came at once, and taking the cup in both hands Jack gazed absently at the back of the man at the grill and allowed his mind to go blank. He ate his sausages, paid his check, and left.

As soon as he was in front of the canvas again, the figure of the boy by the water occupied him exclusively. The canvas thickened and grew heavy, and when Jack left off, late in the day, he was drained and clear and tranquil, and he went down to Dorian's and sat at the bar and ordered a steak and fries. He drank a bottle of red wine with it; and upstairs, he went to sleep on the couch not unhappy, not without a vague sense of hope.

BUT THE NEXT DAY'S WORK DESTROYED UTTERLY ANY hope of a successful resolution. Jack had always in the end to abandon his paintings. That there was always something wrong, something unrealized, became the impetus for the next one, the engine that drove him on. The work itself was hell, for the most part, a perpetually frustrated striving to manifest some ill-glimpsed possibility that was pure and perfect only in the idea, never in the reality. He walked east on Fourteenth Street, shoulders tight with tension and his overcoat unbuttoned despite the chill of the evening. He smoked one cigarette after another. He was filled with despair, and drank for some hours at the Cedar Tavern, where he took solace from the ghosts of dead painters who clustered about him at the empty bar. It was after ten when he reached the meat district again, and, passing the corner of Little West Twelfth Street, he was observed by a group of seven men, three in white coats, seated on planks about a blazing trash-can brazier and sharing a bottle. He went straight into Dorian's, which was packed and noisy, found a space at the bar and ordered a large Scotch. An hour later he was still there, walled up in a dungeon of self as the prattle and twitter of people at ease washed round him like swift waters streaming by a foundered hulk. Whisky is not good for a man in Jack Fin's state of mind; whisky is diabolical: it inflames and enrages, it fuels anger, exacerbates conflict, spreads havoc. They didn't exactly throw him out, but after there had twice occurred nasty little snarl-ups, little knots in the smooth grain of the evening, for each of which he knew he was somehow responsible, he found himself on the sidewalk. The cold air revived him somewhat, and he walked unsteadily down Gansevoort toward the river.

On the far side of Washington Street the old West Side Highway, elevated on huge studded girders, rears dripping and rusted from block to block, dead-ending into the south wall of a building, resuming its empty journey to the north. Weeds and bushes spill from the abandoned roadway high overhead. As Jack tottered beneath it, his passage was tracked by a stray dog, sniffing round the darkened warehouses on Washington Street, and by a figure in the shadows half a block to the south, who followed at a distance as Jack crossed Tenth Avenue and fetched up once more by the river. There he settled himself among the debris of the waterfront. No light yet pierced the turmoil of his brain; the moon was hidden by clouds, and the water was black against the sky. Jack sat hunched on a rock, immobile, with his back bowed and his forehead fixed in the palm of his right hand.

Time passed; and then the clouds began to drift south, and suddenly the moon emerged, to shed a livid, glowing ribbon of light across the river. Something stirred in Jack at this point. His head came up; he turned to the west and gazed, apparently transfixed, at the moonlight on the water. He heaved himself upright and stood there, swaying, on the waterfront. Then he did a most peculiar thing: he began to get undressed. He struggled with the overcoat, and he had to support himself against a post getting his shoes and socks off; but after some moments his garments lay in a heap beside him and the man himself stood naked and shivering with his thick white back turned toward the city. And then he scrambled, crablike, down to the water's edge.

The figure who had shadowed Jack from Washington Street now crouched on his haunches and watched from a dark place down the waterfront. He saw Jack go under—and come up, thrashing wildly, with a shout of shock, as the chill bit into him and sliced through his drunkenness like a butcher's knife! Out of the water he came, the kraken, with his hair plastered across his face and his white slabbed body pimpled and twitching with cold. He dressed himself hurriedly and made his way back across the highway and into the meat district; and the watching figure slipped away and was swallowed by the night.

WHEN JACK AWOKE THE NEXT MORNING, FULLY CLOTHED, on the couch, he could not remember what had impelled him to go into the river. He took a long, hot shower and despite the hangover managed to snort with some amusement at the thought of it. Perhaps he'd intended to swim to Jersey. He scrubbed himself with unwonted thoroughness, though, for the very idea of swimming in the Hudson was repulsive: baptism by filth, he thought. And then he stopped thinking about it, simply banished it from his mind: such things happen in the night, that's all. He put on clean clothes and, his hair still damp and his head throbbing, sat on the hard chair with a cigarette and gazed at *Wharf*.

At this stage it was a painting that seemed to be exclusively about tarred timbers. They floated in a crude, massy heap on a ground that was now more fog than river-sky, a noxious fog touched with flecks of yellow and gray. The leading timbers loomed from the fog with massive physicality, dripping tar like diseased thick limbs perspiring; the stump of one of these timbers had begun to assume the characteristics of a rudimentary hoof, a horny plate fringed by hanks of bristle the same brown as the timber. The figure remained problematic; it had become essential to the composition—a mere black splinter of a thing though it was—but its relation to the timber and the hoof was unclear. Jack gazed at it a long while. From the street below came the sounds of the meat district, shouts and engines. It was a cold day, and overcast. At noon he drank a can of beer and felt better. Then he went out and ate a cheeseburger in the coffee shop, and thought about his "swim." He should, he supposed, have been alarmed at behaving so bizarrely, and so imprudently; the waterfront at Fourteenth Street was not the choicest spot for a carefree midnight dip. But Jack was not alarmed. An ironic snort was the extent of his reaction. Such things happen in the night. He was curious, though, about the chain of reasoning that had led him to do it, for in the cold light of sobriety it was inexplicable.

When he returned to the loft there was a message on his machine. The voice was one he had not heard for three years: it was Erica, his wife.

JACK WENT BACK TO WORK, AND SPENT THE AFTERNOON worrying at *Wharf*. Painting is not a cerebral activity; even as he worked his brain was handling large blocks of information quite unrelated to the business at hand. Memories came bubbling up in clusters, all charged with bad affect. The failure of his marriage was his own doing, of this he had never been in the slightest doubt. His analysis of that failure was not complicated. The superficial causes were (a) his drinking and (b) his painting: he pursued both these activities with such obsessive dedication that no time, no emotional energy had been available for Erica. Why did he behave this way? Because he was, by nature, incapable of generosity, consideration, tenderness and sensuality: all the things a woman wants. He was, in short, unable to love. Or so he assumed. There is a tradition in dramatic narrative whereby the alcoholic always dies. Sometimes he's the faithful sidekick who despite his undependability comes through for the hero when he's most needed—and then, with pathos, expires. Or he may be a hero himself, like Lowry's Consul, a tragic hero whose spiritual infirmity is masked by drink—*"no se puede vivir sin amar"*—and then expires. Of whatever type, though, from the first trembling shot downed you know that he, or she, is probably doomed. Not Jack Fin. Jack Fin represented a new type: built like a bull, incapable of suicide, he would bluster, blinkered, down his narrow alley into a fractious old age. He was the lush triumphant—*victor bibulus*—unrepentant, incorrigible, and equipped with an apparently imperishable liver. The sound of his wife's voice evoked in him no tremor of remorse or regret: it was better this way, better for all concerned. She was in the city for only two days, and wanted to see him this evening, as there was something she had to discuss with him. Money, he imagined.

Something odd had in the meanwhile begun to happen to *Wharf*. As the stump of the leading timber more strongly assumed the look of a hoof, so the other timbers by association became the legs of galloping beasts. The hooded figure hung like a dark conspiring angel close upon the ghostly herd as it came stamping out of the yellowy fog, an eerily silent chaos of headless, bodiless, tar-smeared limbs. From what world had they come? On what foul plain had these hellish cattle grazed? Jack gave it up for the day. He opened a beer. He had arranged to meet Erica at eight, not in the loft but in Dorian's. He was feeling anxious, but doubtless that was the hangover. At least he was clean.

The streets were quiet in the late afternoon. A sea gull cried from the edge of a warehouse roof, and a single forklift moved back and forth on the sidewalk, between wired bales of compressed cardboard and a stack of wooden pallets. Jack crossed the highway to the waterfront, where scraps of black plastic and thin, hardy weeds fluttered and flapped in the wind, and a sudden motion of waves washed against the rubble of concrete and dirt and old tires as a long, low barge moved downriver, far out in the middle of the stream, and the light of the wintry sun blazed up fiercely off the water despite the cold. This was the site of his "swim." He walked out on the landfill, down the side of a long gray hangar in which was piled to the roof a vast hill of coarse dirty salt, for spreading on the roads in winter. Somewhere atop the hill of salt a fire was burning, he could smell it, and he stood at the open end of the hangar gazing up into the roof where the smoke poured out through a missing panel. From high in the salt a figure appeared and gazed down at him. For some moments they stared at each other, and then the other turned back to his fire and was lost to sight. A group of men had been camping in the salt for two years now, living on the meat market's leftovers and handouts. Jack had been up there drinking on occasion; they were young white men, and they probably ate better than most of the city: there had been fresh lobster and prime steak the night he'd dined with them. His particular friend was Blue, a red-bearded hillbilly in a baseball cap from West Virginia. Blue told him stories about life in the salt, about rats the size of dogs and crack-heads who murdered one another with shotguns. Jack always gave him a few bucks, and Blue always spent it on liquor. "We live good up here," he said. "Can't beat the rent." They all laughed about that.

Jack sat down by the river and watched the light thicken over the Jersey shore. Already to the east the sky was dark, and to the south the twin towers reared up amid the forest of high buildings that rise beyond the roofs of Tribeca, all hazed in the last light and oddly unreal, like a film set.

ERICA WAS ALREADY IN DORIAN'S WHEN JACK CAME IN AT twenty past eight. He had had some drinks since returning from the river; he imagined she would find him crumpled and likable; this was the impression he intended to give, at any rate. But Erica was English and had common sense. "My god, Jack," she said, "you look bloody terrible."

"Thanks, Eric," he said. He always called her Eric. "You're looking well."

Then, without preamble, and simultaneously searching her bag for cigarettes, she told him she needed a divorce. Jack turned away, looking for a waiter.

"Well?"

"Why now?"

"I'm going to marry someone."

"Paul Swallow?"

"Yes, I'm going to marry Paul. Don't make faces, Jack!"

"All right, all right. Do you want a drink?"

"No. So there won't be a problem?"

"Of course not." Jack sniffed. He ordered a beer.

"Good. Thank you." Her cigarette barely lit, she ground it out in the ashtray and reached for her coat. She began to slide out of the banquette.

"You're not leaving?" said Jack, rather shocked.

"Yes, I'm leaving. You obviously don't want to see me—"

"Why do you say that?"

Erica paused. "You ask me to meet you here, not

upstairs. You arrive late. You're drunk already. I don't like watching you get drunk, Jack. I did it for four years."

"Christ, Eric, get off it," said Jack. "You mean you're going back to London tomorrow and that's it?"

"Not tomorrow, Friday. But yes, that's it." She slid out of the banquette.

"Jesus." They shook hands and said goodbye. She left. That was it.

QUITE PREDICTABLY, JACK FIN GOT VERY DRUNK THAT night. But he was not murdered, he was not arrested, he didn't even go for a "swim." He was, in fact, asked to leave only one bar, and that because it was closing. The tone of his night was maudlin, and at several points he informed sympathetic strangers that his wife was divorcing him. He was back on his couch by five in the morning, and awoke the next day with a compound hangover. But it was a rule with Jack that a hangover must never keep one from working. He took a shower, and made coffee, and settled on a hard chair in front of *Wharf*. It was not easy to concentrate, for Eric's face, and the sound of her voice, kept rising unbidden into consciousness. But he forced her down and anchored his gaze in *Wharf*. The secret to making work, he knew, was very simple: you just had to be with it until you saw it clear and straight, without illusion. The trouble with a great many artists was that they couldn't accept that all work must fail. Fear, that was what kept them from making good work. Fear of seeing it straight. Not Jack Fin. He could stare into the teeth of his failure hour after hour after hour. That was his strength. In the early afternoon he realized it had to be a bull, and he saw the bull very clearly: it was a beast with massive shoulders, heaving slabs of sheer muscle, and blazing eyes, galloping straight out of the yellow depths of hell, a thousand pounds of concentrated animal fury, timber-brown and oozing tar from every pore—now, that was power! He hauled the clinking paint trolley in front of the canvas and began to work.

All through the afternoon he worked, and on into the evening. He left off at nine, feeling very happy indeed, for he knew he had solved it, that it was going to *come out*. He exulted. From somewhere deep inside himself he'd squeezed out another one—and you never know which will be the last. This is art's angst. He drank not in Dorian's, but in a rundown bar on Washington Street, a quiet bar, where he could savor his day's work, his triumph. He did not think of Eric; he saw only his great bull, his bull out of hell. He stood at the bar with his Scotch, bewitched by his glorious bull.

The boy from the Plymouth was standing by the jukebox. Jack was by this point reconstructing the process by which his bull had come into being. He remembered the figure that had haunted his wharf, then hovered over his cattle, and then been swallowed in the emerging bull; and it was with a shock of embarrassment that he saw the boy now. He felt guilty; he was, in imagination, deeply familiar with the boy, for he'd used him, he'd exploited him thoroughly to reach his bull. They had met only once, when Jack gave him a light on the waterfront, but he found it uncomfortable to look at him now.

"Hey mister," said the boy, coming across the bar to him. "Why you go in the river?"

"I don't know," said Jack, turning on the barstool. "I was drunk, I guess."

"I saw you," said the boy. "Yeah, I saw you go in the river. Hey, I thought, this guy's crazy."

"Pretty crazy," said Jack.

"Give me a cigarette," said the boy. He stood there looking Jack over, grinning at him. He was quite self-possessed, a cocky kid, sizing up the crazy guy who went in the river. He looked at Jack's hands, with their smears of yellow and brown. "Hey mister," he said at last, "you an artist or something?"

"Yeah," said Jack.

The boy lost interest. "Yeah, an artist," he said, and went back to the jukebox. Jack returned to his reverie, without difficulty extinguishing the brief spurt of heat he'd felt while talking to the boy. He returned to his bull. He thought he would call it *Beef on the Hoof.*

Ambrose Syme

AMBROSE SYME WAS A MAN OF GOD AND A SUPERB
classicist, perhaps the finest student of Petronius since
Sir Hugo Crub; but before I begin his tale allow me to
say a word or two on the subject of priest's clothing.
First, it's been suggested that since the collar is worn
backwards, ought not the same be done with the trousers? The idea is less absurd than it may at first appear, for the Catholic priest, if not his Protestant
colleague, is bound by a very strict vow of chastity and
has little call, urination excepted, for a system of buttons the sole function of which is to permit the member to be extracted with ease and rapidity from its
subsartorial crypt. A rather more peculiar feature of
the priestly garb, however, is the sleevelike strip of
material attached to each shoulder of the long black
cassock favored by the Jesuits. These curious append-
ages, possibly a vestigial legacy of the days when the
Holy Fathers had four arms and could distribute the

Body of Christ in two directions at once, tend to flap in the breeze when the priest is in motion and are for some reason called *wings*.

When I say, then, that Ambrose Syme stepped across the quad of an English public school called Ravengloom one very wet December morning not many years ago with the skirts of his cassock billowing about his long stick-thin legs and his *wings flapping,* you will understand exactly what I mean. He was a tall young priest with a long face of sallow complexion and slightly pointed ears, and he held aloft in one hand a vast black umbrella. His arms were like pipes, and had a way of branching from his shoulders at sharp angles so that the umbrella-bearing, or *umbrelliferous,* limb, for example, shot up on a steeply ascending vertical before articulating crisply at the elbow into a true vertical, while the other arm seemed to correspond precisely in the descending plane. His bony knees jerked like pistons in his swirling cassock and black baggy trousers flapped wildly about his skinny shanks. His feet were shod in stout black brogues, the leather soles of which would, in drier circumstances, have rung out loud and clear on the cobblestones; and against this rather dreary composition in clerical blacks and yellowish fleshtones only the stiff white collar stood out with any luster, gathering up what light there was in that dull day and reflecting it back into the murk with a pale gleam; and thus the figure of Ambrose Syme, agitating itself across the rainswept quad.

On three sides of him reared the high, inward-facing walls of Ravengloom, the gray stonework punctuated by serried ranks of narrow casement windows. Behind him two great crenelated towers flanked the main gates, beyond which the gravel driveway stretched straight as an arrow for half-a-mile before disappearing into the mist. It was at the top of one of these towers that Ambrose Syme had his lonely scholar's cell, and for hours that morning the rain had flooded down the gray slate roofs all around, streaming into the troughs beneath the eaves and descending by drainpipes to the gutters below. The drainpipes were old, and several of them clogged with dead birds and tennis balls and the like, so that in places the rainwater overflowed the eavestroughs and gushed down the walls, and in those places a greenish lichen had begun to colonize the masonry. The eastern wall of the quad was the one most heavily afflicted by these fungoid incursions, and against it now there leaned a high swaying ladder. Standing on the top rung, framed against the wild gray sky with a long barbed probing tool in his left hand, was a figure in a black oilskin raincoat.

Were we to examine Ambrose Syme's features at this moment, seeking some clue to his mood, we would find them locked, tense, and grim. We might detect there a quiet desperation. When he looked up, however, and saw the figure poised on the ladder, a startling change came over him. His high-step faltered. He gazed aghast at the poised probing tool and a febrile spasm seemed briefly to seize his long black stripe of a body. Then, as the color rose perceptibly in his cheeks, the figure up aloft suddenly plunged the probing tool into the mouth of the nearest drainpipe, hooked out a soggy mass of decomposing material, and deposited it in a bucket dangling from a nail on the side of the ladder. The purpose of the work was clear; why, then, did Ambrose Syme react with such apparent horror? We cannot know, not yet; but as we observe him resuming his progress across the quad, we notice that his jaw is now hanging slackly open, his eyes are bright with shock, and something less than dynamic vigor characterizes the angles of his joints and the tempo of his moving parts. And it is at this point, as he ducks into the cloistered gallery giving onto Ravengloom's east wing and with trembling fingers folds the flapping panels of his umbrella, that we must briefly examine the mind of Ambrose Syme, a piece of machinery rather more complicated than the simple system of jointed pipes alluded to above.

FIRST OF ALL, A COUPLE OF FACTS ABOUT THE SETTING. Ravengloom heaved up out of the damp Lancashire moors some fifteen miles from a decaying industrial town called Gryme. Originally the country house of an eccentric Liverpool merchant with a fortune made in the slave trade, it had been appropriated by the Order in 1867 and converted into a tortuous complex of cubicles and classrooms, wherein the priests had begun instructing the sons of the Catholic gentry in two dead languages and a Spartan regimen designed to tone their physical and spiritual gristle.

When Ambrose Syme, aged thirteen, arrived at Ravengloom in the year 1947, he was in most regards quite unremarkable. He was tall for his age, rather bookish, and equipped as most schoolboys are with a sort of erotic condenser deep in his loins that generated a steady stream of vividly pornographic imagery and constantly interfered with his reading. Ambrose's father, an Anglo-Irish businessman with extensive holdings in Malayan rubber, had himself been educated at Ravengloom, and knew what boys of thirteen were like. He trusted that the Holy Fathers would harness the boy's impulses and divert them into socially useful channels.

In the years that followed, Ambrose Syme was first terrorized with visions of eternal damnation, and then taught how to displace energy from the lower part of his body to the upper. The technique employed in his case was somewhat analogous to the operation of the common refrigerator, in which liquid is pumped up through tubes to the evaporator at the head, being turned in the process into *gas*. This transformation requires the absorption of heat, and thus is the temperature of the refrigerator's contents lowered. Ambrose Syme did not turn his sexual urges into gas, exactly; rather, he learned to convert them into long, ponderous sentences of a verbose and bombastic turgidity which he then translated into Latin verse, after which he analyzed the form, function, and interrelation of the various parts of the verse, counting the accents and scanning the feet until the heat generated in his nether organs had been drawn off and the primitive thoroughly assimilated to the classical. And this, in a nutshell, is the psychosexual history of Ambrose Syme, a textbook case of compulsory sublimation in the literary mode. In the fullness of time he joined the Order and after a long and rigorous novitiate was ordained a priest and returned to his alma mater to teach classics.

So far, one would think, so good. Each one of us has a cross to bear, and in Ambrose Syme's case that cross was the cross of carnal appetite, of which, it now appears, he was cursed with a considerably larger than average amount. For after more than two decades of successfully defusing his desires by aestheticizing them, it seems surprising that he should suddenly succumb to temptation once more, that he should *fall*. But fall he did, for not even poetry can channel the flood forever; and in his falling he unleashed the full force of his long-dammed lust upon one ill-equipped to repulse it.

"AMBROSE SYME!" CRIED A FEEBLE VOICE.

Ambrose was by this time hurrying along an ill-lit corridor in Ravengloom's east wing. Passing the rector's study his progress was once more arrested. The rector was an old, old man called Father Mungo; for many years he had done missionary work in the Zambesi Basin, then returned, like an elephant, to Ravengloom to die. He sat now beside the window of his study with a breviary in his lap. No lights had been lit, and the room was heavy with the gloom of that damp winter day. "Who is that boy?" murmured the old man, lifting a trembling finger to the window.

Ambrose joined him. Outside the window the ground fell away steeply, then leveled off to a very muddy stretch of rugby pitches. Tramping rapidly across this morass and about to be swallowed by the mist was a boy in a school raincoat. Ambrose could not identify him, and Father Mungo remarked that he was no doubt off for a smoke in Blackburn's Bog. These words produced in Ambrose an involuntary shudder, and the color flared in his cheeks once more.

"What's the matter, Ambrose?" said the rector,

with concern, turning toward him in his chair. "You look feverish."

A large, glass-fronted cabinet stood against the wall of the rector's study. It was filled with masks and totems the old man had collected in Africa. Suddenly it seemed to Ambrose that the eyes in the heads of all these ancient idols were peering directly into his own guilty soul. With a small cry of distress he steadied himself against the desk, and turned away—only to meet on the opposite wall the gaze of a large hanging Christ! He was seized then by an intense claustrophobia; pressing a palm to his forehead he murmured something about the flu.

"Get on, then," said Father Mungo, gently; "and send a prefect after that boy. I shall want to see him."

"Yes, Father," said Ambrose Syme, and hurriedly left the room. Glancing over his shoulder as he reached the corridor, he saw the rector's nodding head etched sharply against the window, the lips moving silently over the opened breviary in his lap.

THE LAND ATTACHED TO RAVENGLOOM WAS STILL LEASED to the farmers who had grazed their sheep and cattle upon it for centuries, and of these tenants the oldest and most durable were the Blackburn family. Their holding included a stretch of low-lying, heavily wooded country about a mile-and-a-half from the school, a damp pocket of the moors which had always been known as Blackburn's Bog. Generations of schoolboys had found in its wild and dripping heart a welcome refuge from institutional existence, and these occasional outlaws would generally gravitate towards the pond in the middle of the bog; for there was in its black depths—its shadowed and unmoving surface, its swampy banks of drooping bullrushes and nodding convolvuli with trumpet-shaped flowers of pale blue—a sort of darkly exotic aura of tragedy that proved irresistible to the gothic soul of the Ravengloom boy; and the nameless lad who had cut so boldly across the rugby pitches was just such a boy. By this time he was over the gate that gave onto the lane leading to the bog and sloshing happily through rut and puddle. The sky was gray, and the rain continued in a steady drizzle. To either side of him stretched the rolling, soggy moors, intersected by low stone walls and scrubby, bedraggled hedges, and over in the east the great brown back of Broadmoor Pike reared up dimly through the misty film of rain. Ahead he could make out the first trees, vague, leafless, skeletal structures whose slender dripping branches he imagined to be the dendroid limbs of some bewitched and denatured army of lost Arthurian knights. As he tramped into the wood and down the narrow quagmire of a track that wound through the soggy bracken he could hear no sound but the steady plash of rain on dead leaves and the damp squelch of his boots in the mud. Gently descending into the heart of the bog, he caught a glimpse between the trees of the black water ahead, and a few moments later he was standing on the bank beneath the withered branches of a blighted old willow. An eerie, dripping silence seemed to lie upon the place, and the only motion the spreading ring of ripples about each drop of rain that touched the dark surface of the pond. The boy smoked quietly, leaning against the tree, and watched each set of ripples become the epicycloid of a new ring, until that ring was subsumed by a third, and it by a fourth, and so on, such that the whole expanse of water resolved to a patterned flux of constant transformation more complex and geometrically perfect than the eye could for more than an instant comprehend. And then, as his gaze wandered over the water toward the mist-enshrouded forms of the birches and willows on the far side, he realized that the pattern was disturbed. A thin stream which drained into the pond amidst a copse of silver birches seemed to be tugging at something caught in the weeds in the shallows, creating a series of swirling vortices that eddied outwards and ruffled the patterned ripples to a turmoil and aroused in the boy an urge to know its nature; so he made his way around the pond and through the copse of silver birches till he was standing at the outlet of the stream; and there in the shallows of the black pond he found the source of the disorder. He gazed unbelieving for a moment, then trembled violently and stepped back into the dripping trees, where with shaking hands he lit another cigarette; and then a voice spoke, and the boy's blood froze and the hairs stood erect on the back of his neck.

"Bird!" Being named, he was subjected; for there, advancing upon him with a bicycle, was a Ravengloom prefect. Bird threw the cigarette behind him, but the gesture was futile. It landed on a fallen trunk and continued to burn, the thin drifting trail of smoke indicting him beyond a shadow of a doubt.

"Smoking, Bird," said the older boy. "Father Mungo wants to see you."

"Look, Holmes, there's a body in the pond."

"Don't push it, Bird."

74

"See for yourself!" cried the boy. And he splashed forward through the weeds to the place where it lay.

"I say, Bird," said the prefect, following him, "it'll be the worse for you . . ." Then he too saw it, and the pair of them stood in silent contemplation of the puffy little body turning back and forth, back and forth in the thin sluggish current of the discharging stream.

AMBROSE SYME WAS STANDING IN FRONT OF A BLACK-board as before him toiled his class of boys, their clever, impertinent faces nodding negligently over their Ovids; and some demon asked: and what use was Ovid in your hour of gravest temptation? And the answer came back: none. Ambrose Syme saw in his mind's eye then the figure with the probing tool etched sharp and black against the sky, and he shuddered. He left the class in the charge of a prefect and made his way rapidly through the east wing to the cloistered gallery giving onto the quad. As he passed the rector's study the old man was still bent over his breviary. He glanced up, frowning, as Ambrose rushed by, then rose and followed him.

Ambrose Syme, bareheaded and without umbrella, reached the cloisters and dashed across the rainy quad, and as he had feared, the man with the ladder had made steady progress along the east wall and clearly would soon be unblocking the drainpipes of the tow-ers. It was into the tower to the left of the main gate that the wet and panting priest now let himself, enter-ing a musty hallway, dimly lit and festooned with cobwebs, at the rear of which could be discerned a spiral staircase. He was quickly on the first metal rung of the staircase and ascending the great twisting shaft, his eyes as wild as his mind and blazing furiously in the gloom. Reaching the top of the tower, he ignored the door to his own small room and instead clambered up a steel ladder fixed to the wall of the landing and pushed open a trapdoor in the ceiling, whence he heaved himself into the attic. He glanced about the cluttered and neglected chamber for a moment; then, seizing up a wooden fishing rod from amongst a pile of ancient cricket bats and billiard cues, he crossed the room, ascended a shallow flight of wooden steps to a metal trapdoor the bolts of which he pulled back, and with the great steel flaps rising slowly on either side of him emerged onto the battlement of the tower. He crossed the battlement and peered over the side onto the slate roof below; then began carefully to maneuver the fishing rod into the trough that ran along the top of the wall. But the mouth of the drainpipe lay beyond the reach of his rod, so as the rain drizzled down upon his gaunt black form and the wind plucked at his hair and his wings and the skirts of his cassock, he climbed over the edge of the battlement and gently lowered himself onto the wet roof, where, with one arm hooked about the outcrop of stone, he crouched upon the slates probing at the dark mouth of the drainpipe with his rod.

Father Mungo had by this time reached the cloisters and scampered across the quad with an umbrella hastily requisitioned from the east-wing boot room. On reaching the main gate, however, he did not follow Ambrose Syme up his tower. Instead, he stood transfixed beneath the great clock on the arch between the towers and observed a most curious procession emerg-

76

ing from the mist upon the driveway. For Holmes and
Bird were returning not by the muddy lane behind the
school but by a paved road that gave onto the driveway. Holmes, the prefect, held in his arms the limp
body of a dead child, and Bird, beside him, was wheel-
ing the bicycle, and thus they approached the priest
beneath the clock like a figment of some ancient myth,
knight and squire mournfully bearing the dead, violated virgin child; for this limp body was the body of
Tommy Blackburn, youngest son of the present ten-
ant. His misfortune it had been to absorb the shocking
violence of Ambrose Syme's fall from grace.

Meanwhile, high above the astonished old man the
frantic Syme still fished for the incriminating little
fetish he had so foolishly carried with him back from
the bog; which fetish he had flung from his window in
fear and guilt in the night, and seen land in the guttering of the roof below. Now he frenziedly flicked up
sodden lumps of dead leaves, aware only that if he did
not find it before the man on the ladder did, he was
lost—as if he were not lost already! And now he had
slithered down the roof, digging and probing with the
rod, and below him a sheer drop to the flagged terrace
of Ravengloom's front. Holmes and Bird plodded on
towards the school, the rain plastering little dead Tommy's clothing to his small pale limbs, his thick green
jersey and his stout gray flannel short trousers; and
Father Mungo stepped forward to meet them. At the
sound of his feet on the gravel Ambrose Syme at last
looked up; and in that moment, as he gazed with
horror upon the sorry procession, the soles of his great
black brogues began to slip forward on the wet slates,
and he clutched for the battlement to which he had

been clinging—*but he had slipped too far.* Waving the fishing rod wildly and emitting a scream that seemed for a moment to swirl about the roofs of Ravengloom like some horrible banshee curse, he turned, still sliding, onto his front, to clutch at the slates and flap with the fishing rod against the slope. No fingerhold could he catch, and his feet, then his legs, slid off the edge of the roof and into the void. His fingers scrabbled furiously at the roof and somehow managed to fasten onto the eavestrough, and thus was his descent arrested. He came to rest dangling by his hands from a trough of old tin. The strain upon his arm sockets was terrible, and the tin cut agonizingly into his fingers. He doubted he would have the strength to hang there many minutes.

IN THE TIME THAT REMAINED TO HIM, AMBROSE SYME became quite lucid. He reflected on his life and judged it, on balance, ironic, particularly the freezing of his libidinal fluids in middle childhood. He turned then to the sin itself, and to his surprise found no remorse springing up in his heart, nor any thought of God, with whom he had ceased to have intercourse after several minutes with Tommy. Instead, he felt that old familiar stirring beneath his trouser buttons, and by force of long habit he began to compose:

Peccavi! Libido non potest curari,
Sed semper ministrari. Ego, perditus sum . . . *

---

*I have sinned. The sexual urge cannot be cured,
But it can always be managed. I myself am ruined . . .

And then the guttering creaked ominously and sagged beneath his fingers, and he abandoned both verse and hope. In front of his eyes, upon the old pocked stones of the front wall, a patch of discoloration formed the exact configuration of the map of Africa, its heartland colonized by a clump of lichen and a thin stream of rainwater dribbling down the eastern side like a perversely backward-flowing Nile.

"Ecce Nilus retrofluens," murmured Ambrose Syme; and that made him think, as the pain in his fingers became almost intolerable, of Father Mungo, who was still remembered with awe and affection by the natives of the Zambesi Basin. The awful weight depending from his fingers was now too much to bear; yet such is the tenacity of Eros that he would not let go. The fishing rod had slithered into the trough close by, and far below, the rector—"African Mungo" as he had once been known—was seeing to the body of the boy while Holmes and Bird ran for the ladder of the man in the black oilskin.

Finally, though, he dropped. He fell straight as an arrow down half the wall, wings and cassock billowing out about him, and then he began to tip, every limb rigid as ever, and he landed badly on his left knee. Death came *instanter,* thankfully; then, as the shattered body settled on the flags like a pile of broken sticks, a drainpipe hard by belched softly and discharged a soggy mess of rotten organic material in which could be detected a little balled-up clump of something white.

The rain eased soon afterwards, and a few minutes later a buzzard was aloft and circling the area. From on high it spotted the tiny figures of an old bald priest, two boys, and a man with a ladder and a probing tool, all gathered about the black-clad body of Ambrose Syme. Off to the left, stretched out upon the grass by the driveway, lay the body of little Tommy Blackburn; and close to the foot of the tower, unnoticed in the voided lump of sodden muck, the spot of white cotton that had once been his underpants.

THE MYSTERY OF THE TWO DEATHS WAS NEVER SOLVED. Father Mungo and the rest of the community, suspecting no evil, found none. Little Tommy Blackburn was buried in the village graveyard, and Ambrose went home to Cork, and there, we may hope, his soul found the peace that at the last eluded him in life. His long bones lie there to this day—moldering gently in the rich soil of Cork.

The Arnold Crombeck Story

ONE OF THE MOST MEMORABLE EVENTS OF MY LONG journalistic career was the series of interviews I conducted with Arnold Crombeck, the infamous "death gardener" of Wimbledon, England, shortly before he was hanged in the summer of 1954. I was a young woman then, fresh from Vassar, and I'd been sent over by a big New York daily to cover the tennis. Sportswriting held little interest for me in 1954, and it holds even less today, so when a call came into the office from Mr. Crombeck's lawyer saying that his client was eager to meet with the American press, I quickly volunteered for the assignment. Crombeck's appeal had already been turned down, and his execution was fixed for the morning of July 17—less than two weeks away.

Now, a woman reporter really had to prove herself in those days, otherwise all she'd get to write about was fashion and tennis. I was ambitious; I was eager to show that I could handle hard news as well as any man—this was why I'd jumped at the Arnold Crombeck story. But how to approach it? I decided that the human-interest angle was the one to go for here. Accordingly, I became curious about the state of mind of a man who, having murdered quite promiscuously for a number of years, was about to find himself on the receiving end. What must it feel like? I asked myself. I thought the folks back home might be curious too, if I served it up the right way. And so, armed with pencils and notebooks and cigarettes and questions, I made my way to Wandsworth.

This is one of the big London prisons, built like a fortress, and you feel nervous about going in; you can't help thinking they might not let you out again. They were quite gruff with me. No institution likes the press inside its walls, and to make matters very much worse, I was a woman, and an American. But the paperwork was in order, and in due time I was cleared. A dour man in a black uniform and black peaked cap led me off through the prison on what seemed an interminable journey, broken every few yards by locked doors. At last we reached a visitors' room with a tiled floor and a small barred window set high in the wall. There was a stout wooden table scarred with cigarette burns, and a chair on either side of it; nothing else. There I was told to wait.

I laid my notebook on the table. I lit a Chesterfield and watched the smoke swirling through the bars of bright sunshine that came streaming through the window. The room was painted a drab green to within a few feet of the ceiling, at which point it unaccountably turned off-beige. A twisted flypaper dangled from the electrical cord; it was black with insects, many of them still struggling in their last agonies. Then the door clanged open, and I was in the presence of the "death gardener" himself.

Arnold Crombeck was a small man, bald, and wearing round, horn-rimmed spectacles. His prison clothes—gray shirt, gray trousers—were immaculately clean, and freshly pressed. The man himself wore an expression I can only describe as "owlish." He peered at me with an intensely eager expression, then advanced smartly across the room, shook my hand, and sat down. The guard took up his position with his back to the door, and fixed his eyes on a point high on the opposite wall.

Now, I hadn't as yet decided quite how I should present Arnold Crombeck to the American public. I thought, if I start by telling them everything he's *done*, then they'll see only the monster, and not the man. But if I show the man first, and then tell them what he's done—well, that's altogether the more interesting approach. So I took careful note of my first impressions.

I suppose I'd expected that someone capable of the crimes Arnold Crombeck had committed would be coarse and stupid. I was surprised, then, to find not only that this little man could speak with wit and erudition on a wide range of topics, but that he had made precisely the same assumptions about me—simply because I was American! That first meeting, then, was one in which we quietly corrected each other's preconceptions.

I asked him how he found prison life. Quite tolerable, he told me; he'd always been a voracious reader, he said, and they'd allowed him some of his books.

His only complaint was that there were no plants. He was, he said, with no trace of irony, a keen amateur gardener, and not to have green, growing things around him was torture. They wouldn't even let him have a vase of flowers. This struck him as a pretty callous piece of bureaucratic indifference. He *was* going to be hanged, after all; he *was* going to pay his debt. Why, then, he should be deprived of the comfort of a few green things in his last hours he failed to understand. "A bunch of lupines would brighten the cell nicely," he said.

He then asked me where I was from, and on hearing the word *California* he became quite excited. He was familiar with newspaper accounts of the last hanging carried out in San Quentin, and they apparently confirmed that Americans were no good at hanging people. It was just as well, he said, that "you've gone in for gas chambers and electric chairs instead." He himself was fortunate in that he was going to be hanged by the English method, and in an English prison. All this he told me with a bright smile, his spotlessly clean hands laid flat on the table. There's an *art* to hanging people, he told me. You have to watch for two things: (a)—and here he placed the tip of one index finger on the tip of the other—that death comes instantaneously; and (b)—index on middle finger—that it leaves as few marks on the body as possible. "You people could never manage it," he said. "You always tore the bloke's head off. I've read Mencken on the subject. Know your problem?"

I didn't.

"Bad noose. For a quick, clean hang, what you

want is not the old 'hangman's knot.' We don't use it."

"No?"

"Running noose," he said. "Absolutely essential. A metal ring is woven into one end of the rope." He made of his thumb and index finger a circle. "The other end is passed through to form the loop. Makes for a faster drop, you see. The ring is placed under the angle of the left jaw"—he indicated the place on his own jaw—"so the chin tilts back, and the spinal cord"—he put his fingers on the back of his neck—"is ruptured between the second and fifth cervical vertebrae. Death"—he snapped his fingers—"is instantaneous. No blood to the brain, you see." He looked at me expectantly, as if to say, even an American can appreciate *that*, surely.

All this, he said, would happen to him next week. He'd be taken into the shed and stood over the drop. He planned to refuse the cap. "A lever is pulled," he said. "The bolts slide back, the trapdoors fall—and down I go! Then, with a crisp *snap!*, my descent is arrested forever. The whole thing," he added, "should take about fifteen seconds, handled competently."

It was hard to know quite what to say. But Arnold had not finished. After *that*, he said, his heart would maintain a gradually diminishing beating for perhaps ten or twelve minutes. "My legs will draw up a bit," he said, "but not violently. I hope to God there'll be no urine spilled, and no seminal emission. Above all"—he grinned at me—"no erection. I have to be buried in these trousers!"

I grinned back, rather weakly. "The prospect of dying doesn't alarm you?" I managed to say.

"Dying? Good Lord no." He shook his head. "I deserve it, oh, I richly deserve it. I'm Arnold Crombeck, after all," he said with a twinkle. "I'm the mild-mannered monster of Wimbledon!"

At this he rose and gave me his hand. "Miss Kennedy, it's been a pleasure," he said. "Perhaps we can talk again in a few days?"

I said that would be fine.

"Good. Shall we say Friday, then? Same time?"

I left Wandsworth in a state of mild shock. Nothing had prepared me for the sprightly charm of this maca-bre little man. I found it necessary to reread the newspaper accounts of the trial, just to remind myself that I was dealing with a cold-blooded killer, a psycho-pathic personality, a man said to be brutal, remote, and indifferent to the plight of others. I found myself dreading the next meeting, but at the same time look-ing forward to it with a perverse sort of fascination. It was with a particularly delicious thrill of horror that I remembered his concern about the state of his trousers in the immediate aftermath of his execution. The man was vain about his own corpse!

There was, I remember, some kidding at the office, not all of it good-natured, about my Arnold Crombeck story. Some of the men were disturbed that I wasn't sticking to fashion and tennis. I realized then that it was crucial that I see this one through, and make a good job of it. Fortunately, my editor was supportive. After I'd filed the first installment he told me that the response had been good. There was plenty of space that summer, he said, for a grisly yarn about a loony Limey. I returned to Wandsworth on Friday feeling briskly optimistic.

And once again I had to wait in the front office for forty-five minutes for clearance; and then the long trek down corridors and stairwells, with a silent, disapproving man in a black uniform beside me, the whole grim trip punctuated by the jangle of big keys, the opening and closing of thick doors, and the intense stares of the men we passed—men who looked as if they hadn't seen a woman in ten years, and probably most of them hadn't. And so to that dingy little visitors' room at the heart of the prison, with its gently twisting flypaper and its bars of hot, bright sunshine.

Arnold was, again, crisp and alert. He seemed delighted to see me. His eyes gleamed behind his spectacles, and he sat down, as before, with his hands laid flat on the table and his cigarettes and matches between them, lined up perfectly perpendicular to the edge of the table.

"How did you feel, Mr. Crombeck," I began, "when the police caught you?"

And then something rather dreadful happened. All the pleasure drained from Arnold's face. The gleam in his eye turned glassy. He said, in a very icy voice: "The police did not catch me, Miss Kennedy. I thought you were familiar with my case."

He watched me carefully. The man at the door quietly cleared his throat, and shifted his weight from foot to foot. Did this mean something?

"Forgive me, Mr. Crombeck. Let me rephrase my question. Would you describe for my readers the circumstances of your arrest?" Christ, I thought, I have to flatter the little bastard!

He appeared somewhat mollified, but the original warmth was gone. He asked me, rather sardonically, if

I knew how many murders he'd committed. I gave him the figure I'd read in the English papers. He said it was imprecise, but that it would do. He then pursued a rather horrible train of thought for some minutes, elaborating on the idea of murder as one of the fine arts. Apparently the notion was not original with him; Thomas De Quincey, the opium eater, had articulated it a hundred years before. Then he described to me in detail the sensations that accompany the act of murder, and by this time I knew that he was simply trying to revolt me. He was succeeding, too, but I was damned if I'd show it. His tone, throughout, was bitterly sarcastic, and I was furious with myself for having lost his sympathy. I kept forgetting that I was dealing—as he himself had admitted—with a monster!

Well, he came to believe, he said, that his "oeuvre" was complete—"adequate for posterity," as he put it—and so he invited the police to "admire his garden." He finished up with an account of his arrest. He stressed the quiet and orderly manner in which it was conducted. He praised the British police force. "I expect if it had happened in your country," he said drily, "I'd have gone down in a hail of bullets, wouldn't I? The idea is most unattractive. And I don't think I'd want to be hanged in America, either, Miss Kennedy. Or gassed. Or electrified. No, a short drop on a running noose, then—*snap!*" He snapped his fingers. "That will suit me nicely. Have a cigarette."

I took a cigarette. I needed it. For some moments Arnold smoked in silence, while I scribbled in my pad. I suddenly noticed how many flies were buzzing about the ceiling of that hot little room; and then I became aware that Arnold was smiling at me! The bile had drained off, he was happy once more, he was smiling at me! "Gardens," he said softly. "We must talk about gardens, Miss Kennedy."

And then, indeed, we talked about gardens—or rather, *he* talked about gardens, he talked about nature, and I glimpsed the delicate flame of humanity that yet flickered in his heart. I did not take notes, and only later reconstructed his general drift. "When I speak of *my* garden," he said, "I do not mean the Wimbledon garden, Miss Kennedy. That was a fairly modest affair, but I left it a better garden than I found it, which is something to be proud of . . . I grew some lovely flowers in that soil. . . . No, when I speak of *my* garden, I have in mind the *ideal* garden. Do you believe in God, Miss Kennedy? Well, imagine God Almighty suddenly saying to you: "You may have any garden on earth, Miss Kennedy." What would you choose? I know what I would choose. I would choose an English country garden. Without a moment's hesitation."

Arnold's eyes were bright. He went on to describe the clipped hedges this God-given garden of his would have, the shady, graveled walks, the bower thick with crimson rambler where he would sit and read on summer days. There would be a pond, he said, in the shade of a weeping willow tree, where goldfish darted among the stems of water lilies, and insects drifted across the glinting and shadow-dappled surface; and set against a dark box hedge nearby, garden figures of nymphs, and sylphs, and goddesses, all in stone. . . . He described in loving detail these stone figures, then paused and gazed at me, his head craning forward and his face glowing, though his hands were, as ever, flat and still upon the table. "The lawn is as smooth as velvet, Miss Kennedy, and the flowers—the flowers!— my garden is ablaze all summer, Miss Kennedy, with sweet William, with irises and peonies, with carnations, wallflowers, and Canterbury bells! . . ."

I left Wandsworth emotionally exhausted. Time spent in Arnold's company allowed for no relaxation, no ease. He *engaged* one, at every moment. It was extraordinarily stimulating; it was also extraordinarily debilitating. I went back to my hotel and took a hot bath, feeling weak and somewhat queasy. That night I vomited violently for the first time since I was a little girl, and I had bad diarrhea too. Nevertheless, I went into the office the next day and filed my story. I was pale and unsteady, and in no mood for the gibes of the men. I was to see Arnold once more, on the following Tuesday. Two days after that he would hang.

I did not spend a happy weekend. I read over my notes and prepared for Tuesday. I would, I decided, write one more piece on Arnold Crombeck the man— build it around his country-garden fantasy, maybe— and then I'd reveal the monster. But it seemed that even thinking about such things was enough to make me ill, for I spent most of the next three days with one end of me or the other stuck in the toilet bowl. I presumed it was English cooking—one of their bloody pork pies or something.

I felt slightly better on Tuesday, but still far from confident. I doubt I'd have felt confident even if I'd been in top form—for in this, the last interview, I planned to ask Arnold about his crimes, about all the women he'd murdered. But as I was once again led down those grim, clanging corridors, I found myself thinking not about his victims, not about all those poor women, but about the man himself. Did death really hold no terrors for him? For now—the chilling thought kept coming back to me—he had less than forty-eight hours to live!

But Arnold's composure was, as ever, perfect. The question intrigues me still, whether Arnold Crombeck was truly unconcerned about his imminent death, or simply assuming a mask. Was it all a *performance?* I still wonder. And I think, in the light of what I've learned about the human condition over the course of a long and distinguished journalistic career, that it *was* a performance. I think Arnold Crombeck was deeply terrified of being hanged—that was why he spoke of it in such obsessive detail. I think that the habit of self-restraint, of formality, was so deeply ingrained in him that he could not express his feelings even *in extremis*. And he *did* have feelings; there *was* a man inside the monster—of that I am certain. In the end one cannot but admire his control; it's very typically Anglo-Saxon, of course, though I wasn't mature enough to realize it at the time.

His composure was, as I say, perfect; but after a moment he said: "Miss Kennedy, you don't look at all well."

It was nothing, I told him; an upset stomach, no more. But he was very concerned, and offered to postpone the interview, although, as he said with a small smile, his schedule was "rather tight" the next day or so, and after that—"how would you put it, Miss Kennedy? I shall be out of town. Indefinitely!"

But I wouldn't hear of it, and after further assurances that I was quite well enough to continue, I broached my question. Arnold got the point immediately. "Ah," he said. "Methodology."

He was then silent for a moment, apparently gathering his thoughts. All was as usual—the guard at the door, the flies, the heat. It was a very hot summer, 1954, by British standards. Then he spoke.

"I have always been a neat man," he said slowly. "I was taught the importance of good tailoring early in life. . . . Do you know Max Beerbohm, Miss Kennedy? A fine stylist; you would do well to study his constructions. Max says: 'The first aim of modern dandyism is the production of the supreme effect through means the least extravagant.' The same, I think, is true of murder."

Like a preacher, Arnold proceeded to develop his text. I was not feeling at all well, and the content of Arnold's "sermon" did little to improve matters. Nevertheless, I scribbled dutifully, mindlessly, as he spoke of his distaste for certain "techniques." "Who can take pleasure in an ax murder, after all?" he said. "Can you imagine the *mess*, Miss Kennedy?"

"Some murders are better than others, then?"

"Oh, good Lord, of course they are."

"Such as?"

"Well, I have more respect for a drowner," he said. "Have you heard of G. J. Smith?"

I had not.

"Brides-in-the-bath man. True monster. Grew careless toward the end of his career; hanged at Maidstone in the summer of 1915. He didn't die well." Arnold shook his head. "Have to die well," he murmured, drumming his fingers on the table—the first and only manifestation of anxiety I ever saw in the man. "I've drowned," he went on. "Never from choice, always out of necessity. There's an art to it; there's a right way and a wrong way, as in everything else. . . . But you know *my* method, don't you, Miss Kennedy?" The eyes gleamed behind the spectacles; the hands were flat on the table once more.

"You're a poisoner."

"Precisely. And it's as a poisoner that I hope to be remembered." He became very matter-of-fact at this point, very formal. "I only poisoned women, Miss Kennedy, and I poisoned them three at a time." He waited till I'd got that down. He seemed concerned that this segment of the interview be accurately recorded. "Do you know what I would do with them then?"

"Tell me," I said. I had read the papers, of course, but I wanted to get it straight from the horse's mouth, as it were.

"I posed them."

"You posed them."

"That's right. Have a cigarette, Miss Kennedy. I grouped them and draped them. I *arranged* them. I derived genuine aesthetic pleasure from it."

"This was after—?"

"After they'd died, yes. I came to think of them as *tableaux morts.*"

He had to spell that one out for me.

"And it always seemed such a pity to have to dismantle them when the sun went down. But one day it occurred to me that I didn't have to."

"Didn't have to what, Mr. Crombeck?" My mouth was dry as a bone, and my head was spinning. I could barely see the pad in front of me.

"Didn't have to dismantle them, Miss Kennedy. Not immediately, at any rate. I could keep them around for a few days, cohabit with them. And you know what I found?"

"No."

"I found I could sleep like a baby with dead women in the house. You obviously don't suffer from insomnia, Miss Kennedy, so you won't understand what this means."

"And then?" I was close to blacking out.

"Oh," he said, "then I planted them. Put them in the garden."

"I see."

"Got all that, Miss Kennedy?"

I had.

"Strange bird, the mind, eh?"

Well, that was the heart of darkness as far as Arnold Crombeck was concerned. He was willing, he told me, to go into greater detail if I wished; but that was quite enough for me. He seemed pleased. He terminated the interview shortly afterward. He shook my hand warmly and said he hoped I'd be feeling better soon. Then he nodded to the guard, and left the room. And that was the end of our relationship—or so I thought.

WHEN I GOT BACK TO THE HOTEL I WENT STRAIGHT TO bed—and stayed there, apart from trips to the bathroom, for the next two days. I was really very ill, but I thought that I'd merely "eaten something," and didn't call a doctor. On Thursday morning I listened to the BBC news. A crowd of at least two hundred people,

most of them women and children, had gathered outside the gates of Wandsworth Prison, and at shortly
after eight o'clock, when the black flag was run up,
cheering broke out and lasted for ten minutes. Poor
Arnold.

Half-an-hour later, I received a call from Scotland
Yard. They told me not to go anywhere, and that an
ambulance was on its way; and within a few minutes I
was being wheeled out of the hotel, with a doctor in
close attendance. I don't remember much about all
this, quite frankly; I was very weak. When I was fully
conscious again, I found myself propped up in a hospital bed. I'd had all my blood changed, they told me, a
total transfusion.

"But why?"

They gave me a letter which, they said, had been
found in Arnold Crombeck's cell shortly after he was
hanged. I opened it with trembling fingers.

"Dear Miss Kennedy," it began, in beautiful cop-
perplate script. "If you are able to read this, then I
must apologize for causing you so much unpleasant-
ness. I did enjoy our talks, but I'm afraid I couldn't
resist the temptation to try just one more; one for the
road, as we say. I've always wanted to murder an
American, so when they sent you along, and you were
female to boot—well, I indulged myself, I'm afraid.

"Doubtless you're wondering how I managed it. It
was not complicated. One flypaper soaked in water for
twenty-four hours produces enough arsenic in solution
to poison any normal person. Simple enough matter
then to transfer it to cigarettes. But you know, the
effectiveness of any poison depends to a large extent
on the constitution of the victim, and if you can read

this then I congratulate you. I've always heard you were a robust people. . . .

[There followed several paragraphs that concern only Arnold and me.]

"I have very little time left, so I must close. Don't forget me, Miss Kennedy; and pray God I don't ruin these trousers, for as you know, I should hate to be planted not looking my best.

"Yours faithfully,

"Arnold Crombeck."

I STILL HAVE THAT LETTER, AND I CERTAINLY NEVER DID forget him. And as for his trousers, I contacted the prison authorities as soon as I got out of the hospital, and learned that for once Arnold had got his facts wrong. Executed convicts are buried within the prison walls, in a lime pit—stark naked. But if he *had* been buried in his trousers—? I asked them. And you can rest assured, Arnold, wherever you are, that your trousers were spotless to the end.

Blood Disease

THIS IS PROBABLY HOW IT HAPPENED: WILLIAM CLACK-Herman, the anthropologist (popularly known as "Congo Bill") was doing field research on the kinship systems of the pygmies of the equatorial rain forest. One afternoon he was sitting outside his hut of mongongo leaves, writing up his notes, when a mosquito bit him. It is only the female that makes the blood meal, for she needs it to boost her egg output. From the thorny tip of her mouthparts she unsheathed a slender stylus, and having sliced neatly through Bill's skin tissue, pierced a tiny blood vessel. Bill noticed nothing. Two powerful pumps in the insect's head began to draw off blood while simultaneously hundreds of tiny parasites were discharged into his bloodstream. Within half-an-hour, when the mosquito had long since returned to the water, the parasites were safely established in his liver. For six days they multiplied, asexually, and then on the morning of the seventh they burst out and invaded the red blood cells. Within a relatively short period of time Congo Bill was exhibiting all the classical symptoms of malaria. He was delirious; he suffered from chills, vomiting, and diarrhea; and his spleen was dangerously enlarged. He was also alone—the pygmies had deserted him, had melted deeper into the gloom of the rain forest. An essentially nomadic people, they could not wait for Bill to recover, nor could they take him with them. So there he lay, shivering and feverish by turns, on a narrow camp bed in a dark hut in the depths of a chartless jungle.

How he made it back is a fascinating story, but not immediately relevant to the events that concern us here. Make it back he did; but the Congo Bill who docked at Southampton one morning in the summer of 1934 was not the vigorous young man who'd left for Africa a year previously. He was haggard and thin now, and forced to walk with a stick. His flesh was discolored, and his fingers trembled constantly. He looked, in short, like a man who was dying. When at last he stepped gingerly down the gangway, one steward was at his elbow and another close behind, carrying a large bamboo cage. Huddled in the corner of the cage was a small black-and-white Colobus monkey that the anthropologist had befriended before leaving the Congo for the last time. He intended to give it to his son, Frank.

Virginia Clack-Herman was considerably shocked at her husband's frailty; and the fact that he could speak only in a hoarse whisper certainly added pathos to their reunion. Frank, then aged nine, did not recognize his father, and accepted with some unease the monkey; and then the three of them, with the monkey, made their way very slowly through the customs shed and out to the car. There were at the time no strict regulations regarding the quarantining of monkeys.

The journey from Southampton was uneventful. Virginia drove, and Bill sat beside her with a rug over his knees and slept most of the way. Frank sat in the back; the bamboo cage was placed on the seat beside him, and the little monkey sat hunkered inside it, alert but unmoving. From time to time the boy's eyes were drawn to the monkey's; they were both, clearly, perplexed and slightly alarmed. Congo Bill muttered as he dozed, and Virginia, stony-faced, kept her eyes on the road.

It was a warm day, and in the sunshine of the late afternoon the cornfields of Berkshire rippled about them like a golden sea; and then, just as Virginia began to wonder where they would break the journey, from out of this sea heaved a big inn, Tudor in construction, with steeply gabled roofs and black beams crisscrossed on the white-plastered walls beneath the eaves. This was the Blue Bat; since destroyed by fire, in the early Thirties it boasted good beds, a fine kitchen, and an extensive cellar.

Virginia pulled off the main road and into the forecourt of the inn. Servants appeared; suitcases were carried in and the car taken round to the garages. Some minutes later, a cream-colored roadster pulled in beside it. The owner of this car was Ronald Dexter. He was traveling with his valet, an old man called Clutch.

Ronald Dexter was a gentleman of independent means who had never had to work a day in his life. He was an elegant, witty chap with sleek black hair, parted high, brushed straight back from his forehead, and gleaming with oil. Half-an-hour later he stepped out of his bathroom and found Clutch laying out his evening clothes. He slipped into a dressing gown, sank into an armchair, lit his pipe—and sighed, for Clutch was running a small silver crucifix with great care along the seams of his garments. A curious-looking man, Clutch, he had a remarkable head, disproportionately large for his body and completely hairless. The skull was a perfect dome, and the tight-stretched skin of it an almost translucent shade of yellow-brown finely engraved with subcutaneous blue-black veins. The overall impression he gave was of a monstrous fetus, or else some type of prehistoric man, a Neanderthal perhaps, in whom the millennia had deposited deep strains of racial wisdom—though he wore, of course, the tailcoat and gray pin-striped trousers of his profession. He was stooped and frail now, and Ronald had long since given up interfering with the bizarre superstitions he practiced. When he was finished, he tucked the crucifix into an inside pocket and turned, nodding, to his master.

"Do you imagine, Clutch," said Ronald, "that I shall be set upon by vampires?"

"One cannot be too careful," replied the old man. "We are not in London, sir."

"No indeed," said Ronald, as the put-put-put of a tractor came drifting across the cornfields. "This is wild country."

"Will there be anything else, sir?"

Ronald told him there was nothing else, and Clutch left the room, closing the door softly behind him. At precisely the same instant, just down the corridor, Virginia Clack-Herman, who was a tall, spirited woman with a rich laugh and scarlet-painted fingernails, was sitting before her mirror clad only in stockings and slip, the latter a silky, sleeveless undergarment with thin shoulder straps and a delicate border of patterned lacework at the breast. A cigarette burned in the ashtray beside her, its tendril of smoke coiling away through casement windows thrown open to the warmth of the early evening. She was plucking her eyebrows with a pair of silver tweezers, and in the bathroom that connected their rooms she could hear her husband shuffling about and talking to himself. With her head close to the glass, the fingers of her left hand splayed upon her forehead, she clamped the twin pincers about a hair. Her lips were parted, her teeth locked; all at once she plucked out the hair; her eyes fired up and a single tear started from the left one. Simultaneously, Congo Bill dropped his hairbrushes, and as they bounced on the tiles Virginia cast a glance at the bathroom door. She turned back to the mirror and prepared to pluck a second hair. Bill's mumble rose and fell like the distant drone of public prayer. Oh, to come back to her so utterly ruined, like one of the walking dead! Out came another hair; the eyebrows arched thin as filaments, flaring a fraction as they neared the nose. Satisfied, she dabbed at her left eye with a small handkerchief and then, still facing the glass, she closed her eyes and clenched her fists and sat rigidly for a moment in an attitude of bitter mortification. But when Congo Bill came in, several minutes later, with his shirt cuffs flapping pathetically about his wrists and asked her to fasten his links, she displayed only warm concern. "Of course, darling," she murmured, as she rose from her dressing table and pecked his cheek, leaving a very light impression of red lips upon the yellowing skin.

"I wonder," whispered Congo Bill, "how that monkey's doing."

In point of fact the monkey was not doing at all well. Even as his father asked the question, young Frank had his face pressed flush to the bamboo cage, in a corner of which the monkey lay curled up and very still. "Are you sick?" he whispered. He inserted a finger through the bars. "Little monkey," he cooed, poking it. There was no response. Frank straightened up and turned away from the cage with his lips pressed tight together. From the public bar below came a sudden gust of laughter. He opened the door of the cage, reached in, and retrieved the monkey. It was dead. He laid its little head against his shoulder and stroked the matted, scurfy fur for a moment. A flea hopped onto his wrist and bit him. He opened a drawer and took out the sheet of tissue paper lining it; in this he wrapped the little corpse, then tucked it down the front of his shirt, crossed the bedroom, and opened the door. The corridor was deserted, and he stepped out.

RONALD DEXTER HAD ALREADY ORDERED WHEN THE door of the Blue Bat's shadowy, wood-paneled dining room swung slowly open and an attractive woman entered with a shuffling figure whose evening clothes hung like shrouds upon his wasted body. Ronald, who hated to dine alone, assumed they were father and daughter, and wondered if he could tempt them to join him. There were no other guests in the dining room; in fact, there were no other guests in the Blue Bat at all.

"Excuse me," he said, rising to his feet with a charming smile. "Good lord! Virginia!"

Bill and Virginia paused, turned, and scrutinized him. "Ronald!" cried Virginia at last. "Ronald Dexter! Darling, you remember Ronald Dexter?"

Congo Bill did not remember Ronald Dexter, with whom Virginia had been friendly before her marriage. The two were in fact very distantly related, on her mother's side, and in the few moments of theater that followed, Virginia recapped the rather tenuous blood relationship they shared. Congo Bill participated minimally in all this, his appetite for "extraordinary coincidences" much dampened by the malaria. Ronald was altogether delighted, and his pleasure was shot through with an undeniable charge of sexual excitement—for despite their consanguinity the two were instantly, and strongly, attracted to each other.

There was no question now but that they must eat together, and so, in a flurry of small talk, and continuing expressions of pleasure that they should meet again in such odd circumstances, they sat down. Behind Congo Bill's chair the empty fireplace was hidden from view by a low woven screen, and above the mantelpiece the eyes of a large stag's head with sixteen-pointed antlers glittered glassily in the gloom of the encroaching dusk. Food arrived, and wine, and Ronald proposed a toast to homecomings and reunions. Congo Bill's hand trembled as he lifted a glass of claret to his bloodless lips. They drank, and there followed a brief, slightly un-

103

comfortable silence. Ronald turned to Congo Bill, fishing for a conversational gambit. "See much cricket in Africa?" he said.

"None at all," whispered Congo Bill, dabbing his lips with a starched white napkin and staining it with wine.

"I don't suppose they have much time for cricket, do they darling?" said Virginia, brightly, "what with all the hunting and gathering they have to do." She turned to Ronald. "They're quite primitive, you know; practically living in the Stone Age."

"That must have been refreshing," said Ronald. "One grows so weary of decency and good manners, don't you agree, Virginia? Don't you sometimes wish we could indulge our impulses with unrestrained spontaneity, like savages?" His eyes flashed in the candlelight; Virginia took his meaning all too clearly.

"Oh, but we must have manners," she said; "otherwise we'll return to a state of nature, and I don't think we'd do terribly well at it."

"Bill would," said Ronald. "He can cope in jungles."

"You must be mad!" cried Virginia. "Just look at the state of him! I'm sorry, darling," she added, laying slender, red-nailed fingers on Congo Bill's bony wrist. "But you must admit, equatorial Africa did get the better of you this time."

"Malaria," began Congo Bill; but Ronald cut him short. "On the other hand," he reflected, "I suppose even the savages have manners, don't they? Rather different from ours, of course, but the same principle— which wife you sleep with tonight, who gets the best bit of the elephant—"

"Pygmies," whispered Congo Bill, but Ronald had not finished.

"Manners are what distinguish us from the animals," he said, "so I suppose the more of them we have the better. What?"

Virginia laughed aloud at this. She opened her mouth and gave full, free tongue to an unrestrained peal of mirth that rang like clashing bells through that dusk-laden dining room. How lovely she was! thought Ronald. Exquisitely made up, perfectly at ease. Her dress was of dead-white satin and cut extremely low. She was wearing a rope of pearls; her face was as white as her pearls, and her lips a vivid scarlet. Quite spontaneously, as her laughter subsided, she leaned across the table and pressed Ronald's hand. At the touch of her fingers his blood turned hot and rapid. He promptly suggested that they take their brandy in the saloon bar. Virginia agreed, rose gracefully, and linking one arm in her husband's and the other in Ronald's, shuffled them off toward the door.

CLUTCH, MEANWHILE, HAVING LEFT HIS MASTER'S ROOM, frowning, uneasy, conscious of some subtly malignant influence at work in the inn, had made his way downstairs and into the public bar. He took a seat at a small table in the corner and nursed a bottle of Guinness. There were perhaps twenty people gathered in the bar—local farm laborers they appeared, fat, sallow people, many with a yellowish tinge to their pallor. They were clustered about a wooden trapdoor in the center of the flagged floor, a trapdoor which stood upright on its hinges, a chain on either side stretched taut to hooks in the opening. The ceiling was low, and spanned by thick black beams, and though the air was thick with tobacco smoke a rising moon was visible through the uncurtained window. And then a weak and ragged cheer erupted as from the cellar beneath appeared the head of the landlord of the Blue Bat, Kevin Pander, a young man but, like his customers, very fat, and pale, and sallow-skinned. Wheezing badly, he ascended the cellar stairs with a hogshead of ale on one shoulder and a wooden crate containing two dozen bottles of beer dangling, clinking, from his white and hamlike palm. His wrists and ankles were bagged and swollen with accumulated body fluids, but he came up like a god, an asthmatic Bacchus ascending from the netherworld, and paused, breathing heavily, at the top of the steps. Then he kicked the trapdoor down behind him and it slammed shut with a great bang. Congo Bill, sunk in a black leather armchair in the saloon bar, sat up in considerable distress. "Darling, what is it?" said Virginia.

"Must go up," he whispered. "The noise . . ." Clearly, the sounds from the public bar had awakened some African memory, a memory profoundly disturbing to the fragile nervous system of the debilitated anthropologist. Virginia, glancing at Ronald, helped her husband to his feet and led him off toward the stairs. At precisely the same instant, Clutch realized with a thrill of horror what was wrong with the people in the public bar: pernicious anemia.

FRANK TIPTOED OUT OF HIS BEDROOM WITH THE WRAPPED dead monkey stuffed down his shirt. He did not make for the main staircase, for he was quite sure that his parents would veto the ceremony that he had decided privately to conduct. Instead he went to the other end of the corridor, to a door with a large key protruding from the lock. He turned the key and pushed open the door, and found himself on a dusty, uncarpeted back stairway. A small high window filmed over with cobwebs admitted what dim light was still to be had from the day. He crossed the landing and began to descend the stairs, which were steep, narrow, and, in the gloom, quite treacherous. Reaching the lower floor, he found a long passage at the far end of which stood another door. But barely had he begun to advance along the passage when he heard footsteps on the stairs he had just descended. He stood for a moment frozen in an agony of terrified indecision. As luck would have it, the wall of the passage was not entirely without a place of concealment: there was a shallow, rounded depression, no more than two feet high and two feet deep, quite close to where he was standing. He rapidly squeezed himself into this depression and huddled there like a fetus in a womb, with the dead monkey tucked in his lap like a second fetus, a fetus of the second order. Thus he waited as the descending step grew louder on the stairs.

It reached the bottom and paused. It was like no ordinary footstep; rather, a slow, heavy clump-clump-clump. To the small boy crouched in his womblike hiding hole, with his little heart hammering fit to burst, it was a very terrible sound indeed. It began to advance along the passage. Clump-clump-clump. Closer and closer. Eyes wide, fists clenched, Frank waited. He needed to go to the bathroom very badly. Clump-clump. Go past! Hurry! screamed a voice in the boy's head. Clump. It stopped. Frank glanced sideways in terror. He saw an orthopedic boot, an ugly big black one with a pair of metal braces ascending either side of a slim white ankle to a stout belt buckled halfway up the calf. And then a head, upside down, dropped into view, its red hair fanning out in waves upon the dusty boards. "What are you doing in there?" it said from an upside-down mouth.

"I'm hiding," said Frank.

"What from?"

"You."

LATE THAT NIGHT, WHEN CONGO BILL LAY HEAVILY sedated in sleep, and the moon hung suspended like a silver ball over the black bulk of the Blue Bat, and a susurrus of night breezes whispered through the palely gleaming cornfields like a ghost, Ronald Dexter, in silk pajamas, rustled softly along the corridor and tapped on Virginia's door. Farther along the corridor, in the deep shadows, another door creaked open just a crack; it was Frank's. "Come," came a voice, and Ronald slipped into Virginia's room. Frank frowned, and then tiptoed away in the opposite direction, to the door at the end of the corridor. He carried in his trouser pocket the large key that opened that door. A moment later he was on the back stairs, and lit by the moonlight glowing through the cobwebbed window over the staircase, he quickly descended.

He was on his way to meet the girl in the orthopedic boot. She was eleven years old and her name was Meg Pander; she was the landlord's daughter. "What's that?" she had said, earlier, pointing at the lump under Frank's shirt as he scrambled out of the depression in the wall of the passage. Frank had pulled out the bundle and folded back the wrapping to show her the dead monkey. She had taken it from him and cradled it in her arms, cooing gently.

"I want to bury it out in the fields," said Frank.

"I know a better place," said the girl.

"Where?"

"In the cellar."

Frank thought about this. "All right," he said.

"We can't go there now. Meet me here at midnight."

"All right."

"You better let me keep the monkey," she said.

FRANK WAS NOT THE ONLY ONE TO SEE RONALD DEXTER enter his mother's bedroom. Two men from the public bar, flabby men with waxy skin and big, soft faces as round and pale as the rising moon, and a predisposition to breathlessness, were lurking in the shadows. They said nothing, as the minutes passed, but they were not silent: the corridor was filled, like a living thing, with the wheeze and gasp of their laboring lungs. Nearby lay Congo Bill, who had returned in the depths of his sleeping mind to the eerie twilight of the rain forest, where huge trunks of mahogany and African walnut reared two hundred feet over his head to form a densely woven canopy that effectively blocked out all sunlight, while underfoot, moldering gently, the forest floor deadened all sound, and a heavy, ominous silence clung to the place, a silence broken only occasionally by the manic chatter of a troop of Colobus monkeys. . . . But even as Congo Bill relived in dream his last fevered journey through that dim and silent forest, Ronald Dexter was rising from his (Bill's) wife's bed and slipping on his silk pajamas. With a few last whispered words, a few last caresses, he left Virginia's bedroom and with a soft click! carefully closed her door. The soft click was succeeded by a crisp crack! and a brief ringing sound, as one of the fat men emerged from the shadows and hit him very hard on the back of the head with a length of metal piping. The pipe bounced off the skull and Ronald wobbled for a moment and then collapsed into a limp heap on the floor. The first man lifted him by the armpits, the second from under the knees, and then they shuffled rapidly off down the corridor, panting heavily, as Ronald's head lolled on his shoulder and his fingers dragged limply along the carpet.

MEG HAD FINISHED DRESSING THE BODY OF THE DEAD monkey when Frank reached her room shortly after midnight. It was a small, low-ceilinged servant's room, massively dominated by the bedstead, a vast Victorian contraption of dark, lacquered wood with an extremely thick mattress and a Gothic headboard all crockets and gargoyles. High in the wall above the bed was set a single small window, and upon its broad sill burned a candle by the wavering flame of which Frank could see, on the bed, the monkey stretched out in a tiny gown of white lace such as an infant might have worn for its christening or, as in this instance, burial. Meg herself was sitting very straight in a hard-backed chair beside the bed with her hands folded on a small black prayer book in her lap. She turned to Frank with a solemn face.

"God took your monkey away," she whispered.

Frank grinned, rather uncertainly.

"He's in Jesus' bosom now."

Frank absently scratched his wrist where the flea had bitten him. A small crusty scab, reddish-black in color, had begun to form there. On Meg's washstand stood a large jar full of clear fluid, and something floated in the fluid that he could not quite identify in the candlelight, but it looked organic.

"We have to go to the cellar now," said Meg. She stood up and stamped her orthopedic boot four or five times on the floor. "My leg keeps going to sleep," she said. "Will you get the candle down?"

So Frank climbed onto the bed and retrieved the candle from the windowsill while Meg laid the monkey gently in a cardboard shoe box lined with the tissue Frank had taken earlier from the drawer in his bedroom.

They made their way to the door at the end of the passage, then out into the yard at the back of the inn. Clinging to the shadows, they crept around the building; the walls and outbuildings of the Blue Bat glimmered in the fullness of the moonlight, and from far across the fields came the muted barking of a dog on a distant farm. Meg held Frank's hand firmly in her own as she edged down a flight of worn stone steps at the bottom of which damp grass and moss struggled up through the cracks between ancient paving stones. Directly before them stood a very low green door with peeling paintwork and rusting studs. Meg lifted the door on its hinges and it slowly scraped inwards; a moment later the pair were crouched in the musty darkness of the cellar, the door pushed firmly closed and the candle flickering on the ground between them and throwing up a strange light onto their pale, excited faces.

Congo Bill meanwhile was blindly crashing through the jungle in a state of deep delirium. He had lost his quinine in an accident on the river two weeks previously, and now the fever roiled and seethed unchecked within him. Delicate screens of misty lichen hung from the branches, and through these he clawed his wild way as brightly colored birds shrieked from the foliage high overhead, and the Colobus monkeys chattered derisively from dappled tree trunks wreathed with vines. On through the damp gloom of the forest he charged, till his strength at last started to flag. It was then that he saw Virginia. She was standing beside a sunlit pool some thirty or forty yards from him, wearing a simple summer frock and waving a large straw hat with a tilted brim and a cluster of bright fake cherries fastened to the band. Congo Bill stared at her for a few seconds, clutching the thick tendril of a climbing liana that twisted about a huge-trunked ebony tree smothered in flowering orchids. Upon the pool the few shafts of sunlight that penetrated the foliage overhead picked diamonds of light which trembled and shimmered in such a way that Virginia seemed to evanesce momentarily and then rematerialize, more clearly than before, still slowly waving her straw hat at him. Then she turned and moved round the pool and into the trees, and Congo Bill, stumbling after her, cried "Wait!" as her dappled form danced away among the shifting shadows of the forest. "Wait!" cried Congo Bill, as he staggered toward the pool.

And even as he did so, Virginia was drifting into sleep, her limbs languid and heavy, her whole drowsy being suffused with the lingering glow of deep and recent sexual pleasure. She sank into sleep, dreamless sleep, and as the curtains stirred slightly in the warm night breeze, a single broad shaft of moonlight drifted languidly across her bed and touched with silvered fingers the ridges and hummocks of the white sheet spread over her now-slumbering form.

FRANK AND MEG HAD PENETRATED THE MEMBRANE OF the cellar. With their feebly glimmering candle they crept forward from post to post toward the center, where they could hear a low murmur of human voices. Toward the source of the murmur the two children crept with stealth and trembling. They extinguished the candle; Meg still carried the dead monkey in its cardboard coffin. They ascended a shallow wooden staircase and squirmed forward along a damp planked platform between big-bellied barrels reeking of tar and ale; reaching the edge of the platform, they gazed down upon the men and women from the public bar, who were seated about a screened lamp, waiting. Barely had the children settled, side by side on their bellies with their chins cupped in their hands, to watch, when the trapdoor in the cellar roof was hauled open and voices were heard from the public bar above. For a moment there was confused bustle in the cellar; and then, with fresh lamps lit, two men descended carrying between them a supine form in silk pajamas.

"What are they going to do with him?" whispered Frank.

"I expect Daddy wants his blood."

"Oh, crikey!" breathed the boy, and in his mind a series of images rapidly unfolded of opened sarcophagi and ghoulish creatures neither dead nor alive. In fact, the explanation for the events in the cellar was quite straightforward, in scientific terms. Clutch was right: these people suffered from pernicious anemia, a disease which, if untreated, produces a chemical imbalance in the organism that can manifest in a craving for fresh blood. It has this in common with malaria, that in both diseases there is disintegration of the red blood cells, though malaria for some reason has never produced a sense of group identity among its victims. This is not true of pernicious anemia. The Blue Bat was in fact both haven and refuge to a small cell of untreated anemics, and had been for five years, ever since Kevin Pander had watched his wife sicken and die of the disease. This trauma had brought about what is clinically termed an *iatrophobic reaction* in the young innkeeper, a pathological dread of doctors, with the result that when he detected the first symptoms in himself he did not seek treatment, but instead began to gather about him a cadre of anemics who, like him, were prepared to live and die beyond the pale of contemporary medical practice; beyond, indeed, the law. For five years these committed anemics had maintained a sporadic supply of fresh blood in the cellar, and there they were to be found, outside normal licensing hours, sipping the good red corpuscles their own bodies so desperately lacked. The Blue Bat's clientele being what it was, almost all of this blood came from members of the upper classes. The fall of the Roman Empire has been attributed in part to malarial epidemics, and also

114

to the effects of pernicious anemia caused by lead in the plumbing. Whether these facts played any part in Pander's elaborate delusional system is not known; the psychopathology of that disturbed young man is fortunately beyond the scope of this narrative.

And so the limp Ronald Dexter was stripped of his pajamas, and then—after his pale, naked body had aroused a spontaneous gasp of appreciation from the assembled company—his ankles were lashed together with a length of stout twine, and the twine slipped into an iron ring attached to a rope which ran to a pulley block fixed to a hook set into a thick beam overhead. Several of the men then took up the rope hanging from the pulley block, and with no small effort managed by a series of heaves to hoist Dexter aloft, and there he hung, quite comatose, and twisting gently, as Kevin Pander lashed the end of the rope to a pair of thick nails driven into an upright post for that purpose. A trellis table was then positioned beneath the dangling man, and upon the table was set a wooden keg bound with hoops of steel.

All this work had produced a greatly intensified respiration among the anemics, and even those who had not participated were panting in short, hoarse, shallow gasps, such was the excitement that now crackled almost palpably in the depths of the body of the inn. To young Frank, on his platform, the whole nightmarish scene had assumed a distinct patina of unreality; as the bulky figures moved about in the lamplight, their shadows against the stacked barrels and massy beams took on huge, monstrous proportions, and he watched like a spectator of cinema, suspended in the darkness in wordless captivation. He was barely conscious of the mounting excitement in the girl beside him as she followed her father's activity. Then Kevin Pander suddenly seized Ronald by the hair and sliced open his throat; and as the young man's blood came pumping out, young Meg trembled all over and rose onto her knees and gazed with wide, shining eyes, her palms pressed together at her breast as if in prayer. Kevin Pander released Ronald's hair and stepped back, lifting high the dripping razor then bringing it to his lips while two of the other men took hold of the violently convulsing body so as not to lose a drop, and the rest looked on with little piggy eyes that gleamed in the lamplight, the only sound now the hiss and pant of their flaccid lungs.

At length Ronald ceased twitching, and the spurts dwindled to a thick drip, faintly audible amid the wheezing. The keg was tapped, and now, his gestures inflected with theatricality, Kevin Pander drew off a small amount of the contents into a glass and, to a subdued murmur of approval, held it up before him. In the obscurity the blood was black. He tossed it down his throat; then, his heavy eyelids sliding over his eyes until he resembled a latter-day satyr, lacking only hoofs and horns, and his blood-smeared lips parting in a voluptuary's grin, he said something that produced a perceptible twitch of ardor in the assembly's collective body. And where, you may wonder—though now, of course, it was too late for him to be of any assistance to his master—was Clutch all this time?

A CELL WITHOUT A NUCLEUS IS A RUIN, AND WHEN Congo Bill stumbled into an abandoned pygmy camp there was nobody there to greet him but a ghost; and the ghost in the ruin was Virginia. She smiled shyly at him from the entrance to one of the huts, then disappeared into its dark interior. He managed to drag himself in after her, and collapsed in the cool gloom onto the floor. Illness, according to the pygmies, passes through the following stages: first one is hot, then feverish, then ill, then dead, then absolutely dead, and finally, dead forever. When a small hunting group came through late the following day they found Congo Bill dead. He was not, however, dead forever, nor even absolutely dead, and they set about nursing him with medicines derived from plants growing wild in the forest. At this time, the 1930s, these people enjoyed an existence which to most Westerners would seem utopian. Utterly at peace with the forest that sustained and sheltered them, they lived without chiefs and had no need of a belief in evil spirits. The state of nature was, for them, a state of grace—a functioning anarchy within a benign and generous environment. Not surprisingly, they sang constant songs of praise to the forest that provided for them with such abundance. They were singing these songs when, having seen Bill through his crisis, they carried him into the *Station de Chasse* on a litter, and handed him over to the resident Belgian colonial.

Had he known what was occurring in the depths of the Blue Bat, Congo Bill would doubtless have wished to return to the paradise he had briefly known among the people of the forest. By this stage Ronald Dexter was no more than a desiccated envelope of flesh, an empty thing—*bule*, as the pygmies would have said; but the anemics were by no means satisfied. When, some time later, Virginia was awakened by the sounds of heavy breathing, she opened her eyes to find herself surrounded by large pale women whose eyes glittered at her with an unnatural brilliance. Without further ado she was dragged screaming from her bed; Congo Bill, deeply sedated and ignorant of her plight, slept on in the next room, reliving the happiness and innocent plenty he had known among the pygmies. Help was in fact on its way, thanks to Clutch; the only question was, would it get there in time?

Yes, Clutch had known the anemics for what they were after only a few minutes in the public bar. He was an old man, and he had seen many strange things in his long life. He doubted he would have been listened to if he'd raised the alarm earlier; so he had hiked off toward Reading, where somebody at the Royal Berkshire Hospital, he felt sure, would take his story seriously. By a stroke of good fortune the physician on duty was a man called Gland who'd once read a paper on iatrophobia and sanguinivorous dementia (bloodlust) in pernicious anemia, and within minutes a small fleet of ambulances was racing through the moonlit countryside, klaxons wailing, toward the Blue Bat. But even as they did so, Virginia, in a filmy summer nightgown, was being hustled across the public bar toward the yawning trapdoor, where, in the darkness below, Kevin Pander awaited her with horrible relish.

IT WAS WHEN HE SAW HIS MOTHER BEING MANHANDLED down the cellar steps that the bubble of suspended disbelief in which young Frank had witnessed the atrocity perpetrated on Ronald Dexter was finally punctured. His whole body stiffened; he turned to Meg, and she immediately gripped him hard by the wrists. "Don't make a sound," she hissed, "or they'll drink your blood too."

"That's my mother," he hissed back. "I must help her."

"You can't."

"I must!"

"They'll cut your throat!"

"I don't care—"

Then suddenly Frank broke off, his gaze burning on the shoe box. Meg's eyes followed his; in stupefied amazement they saw the lid move. Then it was still. Then it moved again, and this time it rose slowly, then slid off, onto the planks, and the dead monkey in its white lace gown sat up stiffly and turned its little head toward them. The two children were barely conscious of the scuffling, of the muffled screams, that issued from the cellar beyond, where the anemics were leering at Virginia and making vulgar remarks. She was not a person in their eyes, merely a blood vessel, a blood bank, to be plundered and consumed like all her kind. The monkey (which was dead but not, clearly, dead forever) rubbed its eyes with tiny paws, and with a small sob Meg seized it up and clutched it to her chest.

Frank saw his chance; he was on his feet and down the stairs, and running at the assembled anemics. "You leave my mother alone!" he screamed. "You take your hands off her!" Kevin Pander, chuckling hoarsely, seized the child, then passed him to another man, who held him still and smothered his mouth with a fat white hand. There was jocular murmuring among the anemics about this, all conducted in a rich, slurry

Berkshire dialect, while Kevin Pander began stropping his razor on a stout strip of leather nailed to a post. Virginia had also been muzzled by her captors; her limbs jerked and her eyes blazed with desperation as she struggled in vain to get close to her son.

Then the trellis was being hauled over and a number of men took hold of the two Clack-Hermans to steady them over the keg when their bodies began the series of involuntary spasms that predictably ensue when the carotid arteries are sliced. Close by, Ronald turned slowly on his hook. Kevin Pander touched the razor's edge to his tongue. Apparently satisfied, he stepped forward. He was not smiling now. It was a tense moment, for it very much looked as though Clutch had failed, that he was going to be too late.

CONGO BILL WAS IN PRETTY BAD SHAPE WHEN THEY brought him out of the forest, and it was generally agreed that a few more hours would have seen the end of him. He had the pygmies to thank, then, for saving his life. Fortified with quinine, he was shipped down the Congo to Léopoldville (as it was then called), where he rested up for some weeks before going on to the coast to board a liner for home. It was in Léopoldville that he bought the monkey. His prognosis was somewhat gloomy—periodic relapses were predicted, accompanied by general enfeeblement and, because of the large number of red blood cells destroyed in the successive paroxysms of fever, a chronic anemic condition. In fact, he could look forward to the life of a semi-invalid, and how Virginia would adapt to that was a cause of some anxiety to him as he crossed the

Atlantic—though, as matters stand at this point, the question may well have been academic. He was also filled with deep regret that he would never again do anthropological fieldwork, never again set foot in the equatorial rain forest. Curious irony, he reflected, that the forest in which he had known his deepest tranquility was the same forest in which he had contracted the disease that drove him out forever.

AN HOUR LATER DR. GEORGE GLAND STOOD IN THE public bar of the Blue Bat with a small man in a gray raincoat. This was a detective from the Berkshire County Constabulary, a man called Limp, and he was smoking a pipe. The trapdoor was up on its chains, and policemen and forensic experts moved silently and purposefully up and down the cellar stairs. The anemics had already been led away to waiting ambulances, bound, first, for the Royal Berkshire Hospital, where they would begin a course of painful injections of liver extract, which was how the disease was treated in 1934. The two men were watching Clutch, who sat at a table nearby with his great brown head in his hands, mourning the death of his master, whose drained corpse lay on the floor beneath a white sheet. Sad to say, Ronald was not the only corpse on the flagstone floor of the public bar; beside him lay Virginia, also sheeted, and beside her lay the pathetic remains of little Frank. Clutch had, in fact, come too late, and the three white sheets bore silent and tragic testimony to his failure. Suddenly Limp removed the pipe from his mouth and, turning to the doctor, pointed it at him, wet stem forward. "He had a girl!" he exclaimed.

"Who?"

"Pander," said Limp. "Pander had a little girl—a cripple—she wore one of those boots."

"An orthopedic boot?" said Gland. "A girl in an orthopedic boot?"

Upstairs, a uniformed policeman was knocking on Congo Bill's locked bedroom door. Slowly the anthropologist was roused from his dream, which was almost over anyway. "Who is it?" he cried, irritably, in a hoarse whisper.

"Police. Open the door please, Dr. Clack-Herman."

Congo Bill sat up in bed, his withered, yellowing face pouched and wrinkled with annoyance and sickness and sleep. "What do you want?" he mumbled.

"Open the door please, Doctor," came the voice.

"Wait." Slowly he eased himself out of bed, sitting a moment on the edge of the mattress to get his breath. What on earth would the police want, in the middle of the night? He reached for his stick, and slipped his feet into a pair of slippers. His dressing gown lay tossed on a chair beneath the window. He levered himself up off the bed and shuffled across the room. Picking up his dressing gown, he glanced through the curtains. The moon had gone down, and it was the hour before the dawn, that strange, haunted hour between the blackness of the night and the first pale flush of sunrise, and the sky had turned an eerie electric blue. His eye was caught by a movement in the fields, and he saw that it was a girl, a young girl, far out among the glowing cornstalks and limping away from the inn toward a copse of trees that bristled blackly against the blue light on the brow of a distant low hill. Tiny as she was in the distance, he could make out, on her shoulder, the little black-and-white Colobus monkey. He frowned, as he tied the cord of his dressing gown. Why was she taking Frank's monkey to the trees?

"Doctor."

"I'm coming," whispered Congo Bill, turning toward the door, faintly disturbed; "I'm awake now."

The Skewer

September 21, 1985. I am an elderly gentleman of nervous disposition and independent means, and I live alone in a rambling Victorian house of which little needs to be said save that it stands close to Hampstead Heath and is colonized by a dense growth of English ivy. This house was built by my great-grandfather. It was completed in the summer of 1856, but he, poor man, never lived to sleep beneath its high-gabled roofs; for in a bizarre accident in the summer of that year he was kicked to death by his own horse. Mrs. Digweed comes in thrice a week to do for me, and I keep a dog, a senile chow called Khrushchev.

THUS BEGINS THE FINAL VOLUME OF MY UNCLE'S JOURNAL, found on his desk shortly after his tragic death earlier this month. You will not yet have read about the case, but as it will no doubt be sensationalized by the gutter press I will present the facts here. My uncle was Neville Pilkington, the distinguished art critic; he wrote the definitive critical study of Horta de Velde. He was found, hanged, in his study, and it was I who cut him down. Let me say this at the outset: I do not concur with the findings of the coroner's inquest. I repudiate Dr. Max Nordau's testimony, with its scurrilous implications regarding my uncle's mental state. I suggest to you that this was no simple case of hereditary suicidal tendency; rather, that Max Nordau is guilty of gross professional misconduct, that he subjected my uncle to sustained verbal harassment, and that the effects of this harassment were so pernicious that my uncle was finally hounded, hectored, and driven to the grave! Moreover—but enough. Enough of this vulgar stridency. My outrage must not alienate your sympathy.

My uncle was a refined man, and a solitary aesthete; and on those rare occasions when he attended art-world functions he always cut a most singular figure. Dressed with impeccable restraint, always in dark glasses, slim and slight, his silver hair flowing over his shoulders, he hovered at the edge of society like a ghost. He had suffered serious burns as a young man, and the skin of his face and hands was all scar tissue. Perhaps this explains his reclusiveness. Perhaps, too, it explains why his mind took a mystical, not to say gothic, turn in the twilight of his life. Like Yeats, he came to believe in fairies; and his mysticism is, I think, evident in the journal entry which follows:

September 22. This afternoon a most extraordinary thing. Khrushchev and I out on the heath as is our wont, making our way down the path by the stream. The light was fading fast and the breeze soughing softly in the elms overhead. Darkness had not yet fully descended, but the trees and the water had begun to coalesce such that the separation of substance and absence was blurred and indistinct. It is precisely this atmosphere of tenebrous deliquescence which sounds within me the thanatoptic chord, I think because to a deteriorating psyche like my own the approach of night signals the imminence of its own impending darkness. At any rate, we were approaching the plank bridge when Khrushchev stiffened and began to growl.

You will detect the maudlin cast of the man's reflections; but what, I wonder, will you make of this?

I stopped dead and peered into the gloom. After a moment I saw what it was that had alarmed the dog: some small animal was upon the bridge. I could see its eyes shining, but I was not yet close enough to identify the species. I advanced, not without caution, but with another step it seemed that we had come upon, not a wild animal, but a child—for the creature was sitting on the edge of the bridge and swinging its legs over the water. Khrushchev held back, growling softly. I drew close, and with a flick of my cigarette lighter briefly illuminated the scene.

To my immense surprise the creature on the bridge was not a child. It was a tiny man, with a well-trimmed, graying beard and an old-fashioned suit of some heavy tweed. He was smoking a cigar, but what was most remarkable was that he was not more than fifteen inches high!

Again I flashed the cigarette lighter. His face was very familiar indeed, but I could not at that moment place it. "Good evening," I said. "I believe we may have met. My name is Neville Pilkington."

"Guten Abend," said the tiny stranger in a high, piping voice. "Ich bin Doktor Sigmund Freud."

Allow me to break into the narrative here and briefly summarize a few comments Max Nordau made at the inquest. Neville Pilkington, he said, had been referred to him after complaining to his physician of sleeplessness, depression, and "queer spells." During these so-called queer spells my uncle would apparently enter a hypnagogic state in which hideous sharp-edged instruments loomed out of a black mist and attempted to amputate parts of his body. These experiences were of course extremely disturbing to the old man, for they seemed at the time utterly real and authentic. He would "come to" after a few minutes, his heart dangerously excited and his whole body twitching and shivering with fright. Max Nordau described these events as "retributive delusions." He suggested that my uncle felt guilt with regard to his own body, and that the sharp instruments were symbolic of self-punitive impulses long repressed. He had begun, he said, to conduct intensive psychotherapy sessions with my uncle, but it seems Neville's psyche was well defended, and staunchly resisted the attempted penetrations of Nordau's insights. The Freud hallucination, said Nordau, was a product of that defensiveness. It was one of the most vividly externalized manifestations of psychic resistance in the morbid personality that he'd encountered in his long clinical career.

Now, the image of Max Nordau blandly articulating this nonsense to a gullible courtroom is one I shall not quickly forget. Nordau is a plump, sleek man with one of those plummy, Old School voices that always intimidate the lower middle classes. He has greasy silver hair which is not cut frequently enough and resolves to oily curls on his fat, pink neck and pink, gleaming temples. He favors tweedy suits and meaningful ties, and when he reads from his notes dons silver-rimmed spectacles which make him seem academic, and further awes the shopkeepers, schoolteachers, and other respectables that normally make up a coroner's jury. My uncle's behavior subsequent to encountering the Freud seems eminently sane to me; but you can perhaps imagine the implications Nordau laid upon it.

I stepped back, brandishing my walking stick. "Stay where you are," I said, and pointed the stick straight at him. The Freud seemed not at all dismayed; indeed, he began to skip along the path, waving his cigar in the air, twirling about and grinning wildly in the gloom, and I felt sure he intended to leap on me like a monkey.

This I most emphatically did not wish, so when the little fellow ceased his gambols and ran straight at me with arms outspread I took action. "Hold!" I cried; then I lunged forward with my walking stick. But to my unspeakable horror, I felt the stick pass right through him—as though nothing were there but thin air!

I need not continue with this entry. Such is man's terror of the preternatural that Neville, and Khrushchev, made for home with great alacrity; and when they had attained the security of the domestic hearth, the door was rapidly bolted and the curtains drawn against the night. And then—and this is a point that was not explored thoroughly enough at the inquest—my uncle did *not* attempt to contact Nordau. Instead, he did what any normal person would have done in the circumstances: he drank a number of large Scotch-and-sodas.

September 23. It's hard to credit the events of last evening. I can hear Mrs. Digweed downstairs, and the bustling of that good woman seems to restore me to my senses. A trick of the failing light; a nervous system fragile and overtired . . . clearly I need to get away. What if I'd been seen? An elderly gentleman standing en garde *on a lonely footpath at dusk, lunging at some unseen mannikin with his walking stick—people have been committed for less! Not a word to Nordau, of course!*

At one point during the inquest Nordau was asked why, in his opinion, Neville Pilkington had not told him of the appearance of the Freud. I shall attempt to reproduce *verbatim* the psychiatrist's response:

Neville Pilkington suffered from a severe guilt complex which stemmed from unresolved conflicts in the psychosexual domain. These conflicts were so deeply buried that an extended psychotherapy was indicated. After only a few sessions, how-

ever, Mr. Pilkington realized, at a quite uncon-
scious level I believe, that if he thoroughly excavated
the areas we had begun merely to probe at, he
would have to face certain memories, or certain
truths about himself, that he had successfully
avoided for several decades. The Freud of course
obliquely symbolized myself and my profession,
precisely what Pilkington was threatened by. His
fear translated into a hallucinatory conflict with
the very therapy that could free him of his guilt—
but to acknowledge this meant to accept the progress of his treatment, and Pilkington could not yet
afford to make that concession.

"Do you mean to say," said the coroner, a dehy-
drated stick of a man with gray skin, "that the deceased terminated his treatment because he did not
wish to reveal his guilty secrets to you?"
"I go further than that," Nordau replied.

I suggest, sir, that the deceased did not wish to
reveal his guilty secrets to himself. His psyche was
castellated, as it were, almost to the point of
impregnability. But hairline cracks had begun to
appear, and fearing the worst he fled. I was no
longer able to help him.

This is how Max Nordau spoke. With one hand in
his pocket and the other making fat, flowing, persua-
sive gestures in the air, his rhetoric mellifluated with
rich sonority in that dreary place, and none challenged
him. The court was not surprised to learn that my

uncle left for Belgium later that day. That would be the evening of September 23.

It is at this point that I must talk about Africa. My uncle was not in fact born in England; shortly after the Great War his parents, my grandparents, emigrated to Kenya, where, in Neville's words, "they joined a clique of blue-blooded colonials who made of the White Highlands a sort of voluptuary's paradise." Life was not easy for a child growing up in that climate of privilege and hedonism, and I fear that Neville and his twin sister, Evelyn, though pampered in a material sense, were emotionally undernourished; and it did not surprise me that after the war—which Neville spent in London in the Auxiliary Fire Service—he did not return to Africa. He remained obsessed with the continent until his death, however, as will be evident from several of the later journal entries.

One curious and tragic incident from those early years must be mentioned before I continue, and that is the death of the twin sister, Evelyn. This occurred during the last summer she and Neville spent in Africa—the summer of 1938, just before they were to go up to Oxford together. Now, their mother had been dead for many years, and in the spring of 1938, after a long struggle with cirrhosis, their father died. With no other relatives in Africa, Neville and Evelyn decided on the advice of the family lawyers to sell the plantation and, after completing their studies, to settle permanently in England. Neville promptly used part of his patrimony to buy a little two-seater airplane, and in the little time that remained to them in Africa he would take Evelyn up almost daily for long flights over the magnificent Kenyan uplands.

One evening, as he was about to land at the Nairobi airfield, Neville realized he was bringing the plane in too fast; so he lifted the nose, to lose speed. He spoke of this to me only once, and it caused him great pain to do so; I did not press him for details, and report here only what he told me. The engine stalled, and the little plane went cartwheeling over the grass and burst into flames. Neville crawled out, very badly burned, and was rushed to hospital. Evelyn was not so lucky; her charred body was recovered from the wreck some hours later. After almost a year in hospital, and a long series of skin grafts, Neville left Africa and sailed, alone, for England.

I never heard him speak of his sister again, I presumed because he felt responsible for her death. It was only a chance encounter a year ago with an old lady who'd known the Pilkingtons in Kenya that led me to doubt his account of the accident; it was then that I realized what he had done on the crossing from Mombasa to Southampton, and why he lived as he did.

September 24. I have always had a vivid affection for Brussels, but my sense of pleasurable anticipation has been rather deflated by the disappearance of Khrushchev. Mrs. Digweed was out looking for him all morning, but to no avail. Even as the cab was carrying me off to Victoria I found myself peering down sidestreets with almost maternal anxiety. Oh, dear! I do hope the little fellow is safe. Now I am settled in first class with a volume of Ruskin at my elbow. I have pulled down the window blinds and removed my tinted spectacles,

It seems, however, that I am to be denied even such solace as the LeFanu can offer. At a few minutes after midnight I saw them again, and I rose from my seat with a cry of despair. It was Freud and Rank, standing on a bar at the far side of the crowded café, and they had been joined by Ernest Jones. They were talking about me, that was clear, for their faces were turned constantly in my direction, and Freud once gestured at me in a rather patronizing manner with his cigar.

The LeFanu is a large café, and by this time it was hot, packed, and smoky. A hubbub of animated conversation issued from every table and alcove, punctuated by sudden brays of laughter and the clink of bottles, and to one such as I, drinking alone and not partaking of the general mood, there seemed a desperate and frenzied tone to the conviviality, a sense that if the lights should fail, if silence should descend, some larger emptiness might have to be faced, some yawning, possibly even twisting, void—the effluvium of mortality was there.

My cry produced silence. Every face in the room turned towards me as I rose from my seat. I shook my fist at the three figments on the bar. I pushed my way across the room, my lidless old eyes prickling with tears of anger and my hands trembling as with a fever. The three diminutive psychoanalysts stopped talking and observed my approach from shrewd and hooded eyes. Ernest Jones twitched his nose at me like a rat.

"Steady on, old girl," he murmured as I reached the bar. I went for him; but of course there was nothing there for me to clutch at, no neck to wring

*and no head to punch. A pair of waiters gently led
me off, and the café was within moments as frenzied
as before.*

This was the third sighting. It was soon followed by
the fourth, one of the most critical in the entire sequence. The drama was beginning now to move inexo-
rably to its grim and grisly conclusion, and Neville, I
think, realized this. His journal entries start to sound a
note of fatalistic resignation; at one point he remarks
that "contrary to common belief, one of the few bless-
ings of age is one's ripening ability to adjust to new
and distressing circumstances. Thus," he writes, "have
I seen my friends begin to die off, and thus have I
prepared myself for the loss of Khrushchev."

He returned to his hotel and settled himself at the
table, where he wrote up his account of the LeFanu
sighting. A great silence had settled upon the city, and
he had the feeling that his was the only active mind in
the whole of Brussels. He was not startled when he
heard from behind him a discreet cough. He turned in
his seat, pen poised. Freud and Rank were reclining
on his bed in the manner of odalisques, their languid
eyes upon him. "Jones," he wrote,

*dapper in a black suit with a white collar on a
blue-striped shirt and a navy bow tie with tiny
white dots, was leaned nonchalantly against a leg
of the bed. As I sat, half-turned in my chair, he
advanced smartly across the darkened room, his
little cane tapping on the floorboards. In a moment
he was beside me, and then with simian agility had
clambered up my chair and sprung onto the table,*

where he planted himself squarely on my open journal, one black bespatted oxford upon each leaf. He had eyes like a hawk, Ernest Jones, and they drilled into my brain like a corkscrew or a sharp-tipped spiral bore. He began immediately to speak, in a low, hypnotic voice, a honeyed voice to which I listened with an increasingly numbed passivity, such that it began to seem that the voice was issuing not from the tiny apparition before me but from somewhere inside my own brain. How long this discourse lasted I cannot say, save that his words, spiked though they were with familiar analytic terms, yet flowed with such a potent and seamless logic that the arguments seemed not framed or constructed by any interested cognitive agent but instead snipped whole and intact from the very fabric of language itself; and thus was I led, by degrees, without apparent block or hindrance, to accept his conclusion, radical as it may appear.

What happened next is rather shocking. Apparently, Jones took up the pen and employed it as a lance to put out one of my uncle's eyes. The final journal entry, written some days later in London, describes how, in the moments immediately preceding this operation,

there was the slowing down of time such that every tiny detail became magnified, momentous and horrible. Now it was the spectacle of Jones removing his cuff links and rolling up his shirtsleeves. Freud and Rank had joined him on the table, but stood beyond the pool of light shed by the table lamp, the only lamp that burned in that unholy room. There was the flare of a tiny flame as Freud relit his cigar. Rank was peering at me intently, and even from behind those great thick lenses his eyes glittered perceptibly in the gloom.

When it was done, Neville stumbled, weeping and laughing, to the bathroom, where he cleaned his face as best he could and flushed the tissues down the toilet. As he stood "swaying and trembling over the bloody swirling waters," he experienced an access of sublime sensation such that, he writes, "I glowed like a molten pillar, and knew peace for the first time in many months."

The heartbreaking pathos of this sentence was not apparent to Max Nordau. Even now I can hear him pontificating in that tawdry little courtroom:

Neville Pilkington was of course profoundly and floridly psychotic when he put out his eye in a shabby hotel in Brussels. His earlier delusions had involved the amputation of body parts, and I think we can safely assume that the identical patho-logical mechanism was involved here. I would briefly mention in this regard one simple Freudian concept, that of the bodily ego, the somatic fron-tier upon which the deepest-spawned of our great atavistic impulses finally and indelibly work them-selves out. On this frontier Neville Pilkington dis-figured himself, destroyed a vital organ. Figuratively, and with the only means at his disposal, he hacked down some great standing thing. I leave it to you to name that thing.

Oh phallocentric fallacy! My uncle *had* no great standing thing! Nordau himself provoked this awful act of self-abuse, himself burst into the eyeball with his beak and destroyed my uncle's vision! Enough. It will soon be over. I will see to Nordau with my skewer. For now let us follow Neville as he flounders through Flanders, maddened and half-blind, towards the end.

"I always carry morphine with me when I travel," he writes,

and in the hours that followed I drew heavily upon the drug. I caught the early train to Amsterdam. It was not an attempt at escape, for though my soul was on fire I knew instinctively that after the loss of the eye I was free of whatever bizarre curse had brought these phantom psychiatrists down upon me. You may judge from this how light-headed I was.

But despite the morphine I grew weaker as the day passed, for the eye was still bleeding, bandaged as it was only by a white handkerchief held clumsily in place by my dark spectacles. I had pulled down the blinds in the compartment, and occasionally I glanced out at the diked and channeled flatness of the Netherlands; and in some netherland of my mind I turned to the Congo, its basin lying on the steaming and humid equator, its forests turning to jungle and its jungles turning to swamp, and swamp the breeding ground of killer pests like tsetse fly and red mosquito . . .

. . . by the time we reached Centraal Station I could barely walk. A courteous Dutchman helped me to a taxi and told the driver to take me to a hospital.

I remained in hospital for two days. The eye was properly dressed, and I received several transfusions. The presence in my body of alien blood began, however, to disturb me, so I discharged myself on the morning of the third day and moved to a hotel. I met Freud and the others once more before returning to England, late one night on a small bridge over the Brouwersgracht. The whole committee was there this time: Freud, Rank, and Jones, of course, and the three others. Ferenczi the Hungarian was one of them. They were playing on the iron railings at the edge of the bridge, swinging on the bars and clambering about the arabesques like little children. They did not pause in their hilarious games when I approached; only Ernest Jones jumped off the rails and came towards me. His face was flushed and his broad-brimmed Panama was tilted at an angle. Smiling broadly, he inquired after the eye; then he wondered if it had ever occurred to me that a hanged man is like a vortex, for his body turns in ever-diminishing circles, and a vortex, he added, has only one eye.

That night my uncle set out for London, arriving shortly after noon the following day. He told Mrs. Digweed he would not need her until further notice, and though she protested "with some vigor" he was adamant. "It's too crowded here," he writes in that last journal entry;

the entire Weimar Congress is with me. Khrushchev has not appeared, and I fear the worst.

Yes, the entire Weimar Congress is with me. I am

in my study now, working on this narrative. I have
closed the curtains, and I am wearing my tinted
spectacles. There are psychoanalysts everywhere—
perched on my bookshelves, curled up in the draw-
ers of my desk, crawling over the furniture—one is
even squatting on my globe. I am infested with
psychoanalysts. A number of them are flying about
the room, for they have wings, filmy brown things,
gossamer-thin, like the wings of flies, and the air is
thick with their buzzing. They're all chattering vol-
ubly, but so far they've not interfered with my
writing. I'm a little disturbed, though, to see Freud
and the rest of the committee standing under one of
the African maps talking about me again. Ernest
Jones has got some cord.

I it was who found him. I remember that when the
call came through from a distraught Mrs. Digweed,
saying that though he was very unwell, and his head
was heavily bandaged, my uncle had *dismissed* her, I
was turning a skewer over in my fingers, a metal
skewer for pinning meat. I remember that I allowed
the light to glint upon the facets of its sharpened point
and catch the ridges of its twisting thread as I prom-
ised Mrs. Digweed I would take a cab to Hampstead
as soon as I could get away.

The light was fast failing when I came through the
garden, and a great stillness had settled on the house.
The front door was open, and I crossed the hallway
and knocked on the study door. There was no answer,
so I entered.

The study could really be called a library, and the
upper shelves of the bookcases are reached by a spiral

staircase of wrought iron which gives onto a gallery. The railing of this gallery is also of wrought iron, and to it Neville had attached the cord. The room was dark, for he had drawn the curtains, but the windows were open, and a breeze from the heath crept in and gently turned Neville where he dangled. He had removed the dressings from his eye, and I glimpsed them scattered across his desk at the far end of the room. I righted the fallen chair beneath him, and stood upon it to cut him down with a kitchen knife. I loosened and removed the noose from his bruised throat and opened the collar of his shirt.

What I did next may surprise you; but I had, as I mentioned earlier, for a year known the truth about the airplane crash and its effects upon my uncle's style of life, indeed about his very identity; and I think you will agree I was justified in committing what in different circumstances might have been an unpardonable breach of good manners: I undressed him. And as I removed his garments I remarked again the quality of the materials he wore, and the fineness of their cut. Carefully I placed his dark suit upon the chair, and then the gaily patterned silk cravat, the white silk shirt . . . I had locked the study door and turned on all the lights. My uncle lay naked on the floor, and I marveled then at the deceit that had been practiced for so many years. The skin of face and hands still bore testimony to the flames of that airplane wreck: it was stretched horribly tight and shiny, it was hairless and unlined. His eyes had no lashes and no brows, and his mouth had no lips. I removed the expensive toupée, flowing silver, which concealed his baldness. These, of course, were the old wounds, the disfigurement he had spent his life with, which had constrained him to darkened rooms, seclusion, a profession of private, aesthetic pleasure, an existence celibate and withdrawn. None of this surprised me, nor did the suppurating wound to the right eye. I was not even surprised that the body lying before me was not the body of Neville Pilkington.

It was not the body of Neville Pilkington. It was, rather, the body of a slender old woman. For it was Neville who died in that burning wreck at Nairobi airfield in 1938. Evelyn had survived, and on the transatlantic crossing had assumed her brother's identity, for only thus could she transcend the most debilitating disfigurement of all, her womanhood, and make something of the suddenly narrowed range of possibilities that life offered her. I attempted to persuade the coroner that none of this be brought out at the inquest, out of consideration for my uncle's distinguished reputation, but I was not successful. Nordau did not learn of it until quite late in the day. His reaction to the revelation is of no interest to me at this point; an eye for an eye, I say.

Marmilion

I

HAVE YOU EVER EATEN MONKEY? THE CAJUNS HAVE long considered Louisiana spider monkey a great delicacy. I should know: my husband was a Cajun. They serve it in the traditional manner, heavily spiced with Tabasco. It's probably for this reason that the creatures move so soundlessly; all you hear is an occasional soft "swoosh" as they swing through the trees, and then the tell-tale patter of falling water droplets. I was once lucky enough to observe a group of them gathered for the night. What a charming spectacle of domestic tranquility they presented! Clustered along a stout bough, they were engaged in mutual grooming when I came drifting down the bayou. I saw them all huddled together, with their tails twined and dangling beneath the branch in a great thick furry knot. It's been suggested that tail twining enhances balance, but the primary function, in my opinion, is social. Then they went to sleep, and I shot them—with my camera.

Slavers brought them up from Brazil in the 18th century, is my conjecture. When the ships docked at New Orleans, a few of the creatures slipped off into the wilderness and adapted to conditions there. Nature was bountiful and predators few; in fact, their only real predator is Man, which accounts, as I say, for their shyness today and the infrequency of sightings. But they're there, all right, way back in the dankest region of the Charenton Swamp, and all you need is a boat, and a great deal of patience, and you'll find them. I did; I went out to photograph them for a book called *Our Endangered Species*. It was in the course of this assignment that I first laid eyes on Marmilion.

Marmilion! How sweet the sound—and yet . . . !

I came upon it one warm evening in early September after crossing a blind lake. I had located through my binoculars a wharf on the far shore, and I hoped to find somewhere nearby a fisherman's shack in which to spend the night. The water was as flat and still as a sheet of glass; behind me the ripples from the boat spread out in long furrows, and only the buzz of the outboard broke the deep silence of the evening. On every side the water was fringed with trees, black against the crimson-streaked sunset.

I reached the far shore. After securing the boat I clambered up the levee and found myself, to my astonishment, at the foot of a great avenue of spreading oaks, from the branches of which hung sheets of fleecy, drifting moss. At the far end, white and shining, stood a pair of pillars flanking the deep-set doorway of what appeared to be a large plantation house. The avenue was thick with shadows and formed a sort of arboreal tunnel. The glimpse of those shining pillars was strangely dramatic, in that lonely place. I shouldered my pack and set off into the obscurity.

It was indeed a plantation house, a massive structure in the Greek Revival style, though in a state of advanced decay. It stood in the center of a patch of cleared ground, and the last light caught it in such a way that the pillars literally *glowed* against the darkened galleries, with such a lovely soft luminosity that they seemed almost to be immanent with a life of their own. Everything was disintegrating but for a pair of stout brick chimneys, thrusting up through the rafters on either side.

A feeling of great desolation clung to the house, but I decided nonetheless to shelter for the night beneath its roof, such as it was; and coming again to the front, I ascended a short flight of crumbling steps, crossed the lower gallery, and so over the threshold.

I am not a superstitious woman. But as soon as I crossed that threshold I felt something in the house react to my presence, and I stood dead still. But nothing stirred, nothing at all, and after a few moments I went cautiously forward into the gloom.

It was foul with the smell of nesting rodents and rotting plaster. Directly ahead of me, at the far end of the hallway, reared what had once been a grand staircase. I turned off into the front room, which was full of dust and shadows, and in which I found an open fireplace with tall brick pillars on either side. I dared not use it, for fear of setting ablaze the rubbish with which the chimney was undoubtedly clogged. I built a fire on the hearth instead, and cooked a simple supper. Then I leaned my back against the bricks and drank my bourbon in the firelight.

By this time it was completely dark outside. The birdsong of the evening had died away, and the only sounds were those of the insects, a sort of low, steady hiss produced by the rubbing together of thousands of gossamer wings. Nothing else.

The fire burned down, and I must have drifted off. Then suddenly I was wide awake, frozen with fear and with every sense straining into the darkness. The insects had ceased their hissing, and a profound silence lay upon the house. And then I heard it: a scratching sound, close to my head. It lasted for a few seconds, and then fell silent. It was like a nail being scraped by a very feeble hand against a brick. Slowly my terror subsided. The sound persisted, intermittently, for about an hour. By that time I was not so much frightened as perplexed. Was there some sort of creature in the chimney? Was it—absurd question—the creature that had stirred when I crossed the threshold at dusk?

Before I left the house the next morning I crawled into the fireplace and lit a match. The flame threw a brief flickering glow upon blackened bricks crusted with the droppings of birds and bats. A couple of feet above my head the flue sloped away sharply, leaving me only an oblique glimpse of the mouth of the chimney. I crawled out again, still puzzled, and made my way back down the oak alley, where sunlight sifted through the murmuring leaves and splashed in golden puddles on the grass. I was soon upon the water once more, and heading back toward the Charenton Swamp, and its elusive simian residents. I was ill at ease the rest of the day, and had scant success with the monkeys. You see, I had the bizarre impression that something had been trying to *communicate* with me in the night.

II

When I got back to New Orleans I spent a morning finding out what I could about the ruined house. Its name, I discovered, was Marmilion, and it was built by a planter called Randolph Belvedere. Randolph had settled the land in 1820 and founded a great fortune on sugar; then in middle age he became a prominent figure in Louisiana politics. A stout man, he was apparently endowed with huge reserves of energy and imagination, and Marmilion proudly reflected his appetite for ostentatious splendor. By the time the house was finished, he had spent six years and $100,000 on it. All the building materials were manufactured on the spot, the bricks baked from local river clay and the great framing timbers cut by slaves from stands of giant cypress in the Charenton Swamp. The furniture was imported from Europe, and was said to have cost as much as the house itself.

Randolph did not have a large family, which struck me as unusual, given the man's temperament and class. Perhaps the delicacy of his wife, Camille, was the reason. She had been a legendary Creole belle, and apparently retained into old age a petite and fragile beauty. I was intrigued to learn that her correspondence with a sister, Mathilde, in Virginia, had survived, and was stored in the Louisiana State Archives, in Baton Rouge; and I resolved that when I next visited the state capital I would look them up, those letters of the long-dead mistress of Marmilion.

But in the meantime, the publishers of *Our Endangered Species* were so impressed with the work I had done that they decided it merited a book of its own, to be called *The Spider Monkeys of Louisiana*. I was delighted, if for no other reason than that it justified another visit to Marmilion. For my casual interest in the old ruin was becoming, I could feel it, somewhat obsessive; you see, I had come upon a very curious fact about Randolph Belvedere's death—the fact that nobody knew anything about it.

What happened was this: late one afternoon in the summer of 1860 a stranger galloped up to the front door of Marmilion and, without dismounting, announced to a houseboy that he must speak to the master. Randolph was doing plantation accounts in his study; he came to the door in his shirtsleeves, and there the two men whispered together for some minutes. Then Randolph called for his horse, and without a word to anyone, without even taking his coat and hat, he rode away with the stranger. He was never seen again.

III

It did not take me long to find a pretext for going to Baton Rouge; and once there, it did not take me long to realize that Camille Belvedere was, like the wives of so many planters in the Old South, a deeply unhappy woman. (Perhaps this accounts for my intuitive attraction to her.) *"These lines,"* she wrote in one of the last letters to Mathilde, *"are the effusions of a pen directed by the Hand of a Woman whose life has been occupied solely with drudgery."* Much of the correspondence concerns the unending round of domestic chores that were the lot of the plantation mistress, and with those I need not weary you. What also emerges is that Randolph was away for long periods, and to combat Camille's "disposition to despondency" the family physician, a man called Oscar de Trot, prescribed laudanum—tincture of opium—the effects of which were little understood at the time. In a letter written several months before her husband's disappearance, Camille tells Mathilde: *"I resort nightly to a liberal dose of the black drops. It so relieves my mind, I fear it is impossible for me to exist in tolerable comfort without it."*

My sympathy for the woman was immeasurably strengthened when I read those lines.

Neither of her children, it appears, provided any "tolerable comfort" to Camille. Her daughter, Lydia, was thirty-four and unmarried when Randolph rode away; Camille refers to her always as "poor Lydia." In 1846, at the age of twenty, she had loved a man called Simon Grampus Lamar, whom Randolph, however, forbade her to marry. One night Simon and Lydia eloped. In the course of their flight to Natchez they encountered a flooded stream, and Simon—a gallant fellow, but lacking, unfortunately, both money and land—carried Lydia across in his arms. Six weeks later he was dead of pneumonia, and Lydia never recovered from the shock.

She returned to Marmilion and assumed spinsterhood. It was clear to all that never again would passion touch her, and no suitor ever came calling on Miss Lydia again. She drifted about the plantation like a ghost, entirely immured in her melancholy; and the disappearance of her father had no apparent effect on her at all.

IV

Lydia's profound lethargy was quite clearly the result of a broken heart; but what are we to think of her brother, William? In the summer of 1860 William was thirty-two years old, a fat, idle, ill-tempered, and dissolute man who seldom left the plantation; and in the face of Camille's anguish at Randolph's sudden disappearance he affected a careless nonchalance that "grievously vex'd and plagued" his mother. He rarely appears in the letters, and this in itself is odd. I would hazard that he had been a difficult boy; the task of rearing him would have fallen largely on Camille's shoulders, and no doubt the relationship of mother and son began to deteriorate at an early stage. (I should know; I've had a son of my own.) Southern society has always been rigidly patriarchal, and it must have been clear to young William that his mother's authority was by no means absolute. He realized that she was merely carrying out Randolph's orders, and this aroused in him a contemptuous defiance. In fact, it soon becomes clear that William's personality was a warped and stunted thing, and as he grew older, and became conscious of his moral defects, we can be fairly sure that he lashed out at anyone or anything weaker than himself. The slaves hated him; horses reared and dogs slunk off at his approach. Randolph Belvedere was deeply disappointed in the son upon whom he had hoped to found a dynasty, and no doubt tormented himself with the thought that it was his fault William had turned out as he had. But be that as it may, the upshot was that when her husband disappeared, Camille had no one to turn to but Dr. de Trot and his ready supply of "black drops."

And then, in January 1861, Louisiana seceded from the Union. Three months later Fort Sumter was shelled, and the War Between the States began.

V

I'm what they call in the business a monkey woman. I can photograph anything, but it's monkeys I'm best at and monkeys I've built my reputation on. I owe a lot to monkeys; and helping to publicize the plight of an endangered species like the Louisiana spiders is my attempt to repay some part of that debt. I am, incidentally, utterly opposed to the eating of monkeys.

I am also a Southerner, and like all Southerners I'm obsessed with history. But unlike most, I'm not interested in glory and romance. I'm not interested in resurrecting the Old South in a hazy splendor that far outshines the historical reality. Nor do I cling to the Lost Cause. The Old South is to me an example of a society dedicated to the greatest good for the smallest number. Endorsing such a society I consider the moral equivalent of eating monkeys.

Have you ever noticed, for example, how the

slaveowners of the Old South emulated Classical Antiquity? They copied the architecture of ancient Greece and named their slaves after Roman statesmen. Like the Romans they also made sure the women stayed at home and had no control over their own affairs. The Southern gentleman who "sheltered" and "protected" his women—those fragile blossoms, spotless as doves —in fact shackled them; in a very real sense they were slaves, and that young William Belvedere should have detected this, and sought to exploit it, doesn't surprise me in the least; he was merely imitating his father.

The war changed all that. The war turned everything upside down. Randolph was gone, and William, lacking any inclination to take up arms for the cause, took to his bed with a "nervous fatigue" instead. Lydia Belvedere remained mired in apathetic melancholy, and all the slaves deserted save one, a taciturn fellow called Caesar. Upon his shoulders, and Camille's, now rested Marmilion's fate. Many of the great houses had been burned to the ground by the advancing Union army; how could these two, the woman and the slave, hope to turn back such an implacable foe?

It is with this tantalizing question that Camille's correspondence with Mathilde abruptly ceases. No explanation was available; simply, there were no more letters. Imagine my frustration. After three days spent deciphering Camille's spidery hand in a dusty, subterranean reading room—after immersing myself in the intimate details of her day-to-day existence, and constructing a plausible picture of her unhappy family— just as she faces the major crisis of her life, the letters stop. The source dries up. It was not to be borne. I walked the shady streets of Baton Rouge like a woman demented. One question alone burned in my brain: what happened next?

Late that night, as I sat, by myself, in a little bar on Pinel Street, an idea made its tentative way into the parlor of consciousness. I entertained it; grew warm over it; and went to bed nursing a small flame of hope. The next morning, early, I again presented myself at the Archives and asked, with beating heart, to see the letters of Dr. Oscar de Trot. The archivist came back shaking his head. My heart sank. There were no such letters. There were, however, the doctor's journals; but they were kept in New Orleans.

I left within the hour.

VI

How did Caesar and Camille turn back the Union army? With charm and hospitality—the old Southern virtues. When the inevitable troop of soldiers appeared, Camille was ready for them. The officers were treated as honored guests; they slept in the beds that Randolph had imported from Paris, drank the finest wines in his cellar, dined on wild duck, she-crab, and roast quail. Quite predictably they looted the furniture and plundered the storehouse; but when they rode away Marmilion was still standing, intact but for a few smashed window shutters and a broken pillar by the fireplace. William was in a state of collapse, for he had feared for his life every hour the Northerners were under his roof; and Lydia had been rather roughly handled by a drunken captain from New Jersey one evening. But otherwise there was no damage done. Camille handled the situation superbly, wrote the doctor. *"She rose to the occasion fully mindful of the responsibility she bore both toward her children and toward her house. She is indeed a plucky little woman, a woman of unsuspected fortitude."* Patronizing ass.

Marmilion survived the war; but when it ended, the "plucky little woman's" troubles were far from over. The South lay prostrate, exhausted, a wasteland across which roamed bands of desperate men—landless farmers, liberated slaves, and various shabby remnants of the Confederate army. On several occasions Marmilion was visited by such scavengers. Each time, Camille appeared at the front door and shouted at them to get away, if they valued their lives. Her words at first had no effect; but when she told them that the house had been used by Union forces as a yellow fever hospital, they soon drifted off. Camille went back inside—where Caesar was waiting with a loaded shotgun, as a defense of last resort.

VII

As you see, I wasted no time in getting at de Trot's journals. I often tell people that the secret to locating monkeys in the wild is to think like a monkey. It was the same with those journals; it was all a question of *sympathetic imagination.* For to construct a cohesive and plausible chain of events from partial sources like letters and journals requires that numerous small links must be forged—sometimes from the most slender of clues—and each one demands an act of intuition. It's a project fraught with risk, but it's the only means we have for constructing a credible representation of historical reality.

Take William. It was for him, now, that Oscar de Trot supplied laudanum, Camille having abandoned the habit soon after Randolph's disappearance. William, we may be sure, was by this stage little better than a parasite, providing nothing of moral or material value to Marmilion. He was tolerated, I would guess, only because he was Camille's child, and a Belvedere; precisely the same could be said of Lydia, though she did manage some needlework, and now, it appeared, might even be instrumental in propagating that curious little society inhabiting Marmilion. The one blessing, you see, that Lydia's apathy had bestowed was that it enabled her to suffer the war less traumatically than others of her class. In fact, apart from the incident with the officer from New Jersey, the war did not touch her at all. Nothing did. It was for this reason that she responded with compliance to the sexual attentions of Caesar.

This development I quickly gleaned from de Trot's journals. You may imagine the doctor's emotions as he records the disgraceful information. Imagine, then, his utter horror when Camille subsequently informed him that her daughter was *pregnant* by Caesar!

As for William, when he heard the news he became hysterical. It was probably the last straw; for I'm sure he was aware, at least to some extent, of just how wide was the gulf between himself and the sort of man his father had been. Perhaps, with the laudanum, he still maintained illusions about himself, rationalized his failure in some manner. But the news that his sister had been impregnated by Caesar—whom William still considered a *slave*—would have punctured those illusions and revealed to him just how low he had sunk: that he could permit his own sister, under his own roof . . . but I hypothesize. The fact is, William became hysterical and went after Caesar with a bullwhip. It was probably the first time since Randolph's day that he had attempted to exercise authority in Marmilion; and it was a fiasco. Dr. de Trot tells us that William—who was very overweight—came upon Caesar behind the house, and attempted to thrash him there. Without difficulty Caesar took the whip from him, and then lashed him with it three or four times before the fat man went howling like a child back into the house, to his mother, who was the only one who could have persuaded Caesar to desist from inflicting a punishment that had long been deserved. It seems that from then on, William's pathetic lassitude began to take an increasingly malicious turn, and the object of the new flame of hatred that smoldered in him was, of course, Caesar.

VIII

The time came for me to return to the Charenton Swamp and shoot more monkeys. I've told you my technique for locating the timorous creatures, and on this occasion I expended more than my usual amount of sympathetic imagination; but for some reason they eluded me completely. Perhaps I expended *too much* sympathetic imagination, if such a thing is possible. Anyway, I crossed the blind lake and then for hours I drifted through the swamp, but not once did that sudden stirring in the treetops, that soft "swoosh," alert me to their presence. I passed through one of the weird dead forests of Louisiana—the trees turned to gaunt skeletal frames, and the moss hanging from the branches in strips and sheets, all mirrored in the glassy still waters of the aimlessly wandering bayou. By late afternoon the failure to find any monkeys had somewhat dispirited me, and I consoled myself with a few artful shots of dead, moss-draped swamp maples rising from the quiet water. In the Louisiana climate, outdoor exposures have to be relatively heavy, as the high percentage of water vapor in the air acts to absorb and scatter light. It is the same light-absorbing quality that enables the moss effectively to kill off entire forests.

I returned to Marmilion at sunset. In the light of what I had learned about the Belvederes, I was intrigued, as you might imagine, to reenter the theater in which those strange and tragic lives had been enacted. Emerging from the oak alley, however, I was momentarily startled by the sharply defined profiles of the chimneys. How sinister they looked against the darkening sky, rising up quite blackly on either side of the house—which in some subtle way seemed unwelcoming this time, malevolent even—though doubtless my own ill-temper, the weather—which was cloudy and windy—and, in retrospect, the events of the night all conspired to influence my memory of those moments before I entered Marmilion again.

It was the worst night of my life. God alone knows what was up that chimney, but when darkness had fallen, and the wind came up, there was a wailing fit to wake the dead. Not until the first pale gleam of day came creeping through the shutters, which had wheeled and slammed on their hinges all night, did I manage to drift off for an hour or so; the rest of that night I sat up in my sleeping bag, with my back against the pillar, in a state of gradually intensifying unease, as what at first had seemed simply the eerie sounds that the wind always produces in an extensive chimney system slowly turned into a sustained shriek, as of some being in terrible, unending agony; and when it was at its fiercest, and the shutters were banging and from everywhere around me came howls and whimpers and groans—then it was that I seemed to hear, above and beyond it all, the scratching of that infernal nail. That was the worst moment of all. By then the rain had started—I could hear it drumming on the corrugated tin, and dripping through the ceiling—and from somewhere so close that I even began to think it came from inside my own skull, that hideous sound kept grinding and scraping away, on and on through the wildest hours of the night.

When the dawn came the wind died a little and, as I say, I dozed off for an hour or so. I awoke desperately tired, and felt as though I'd barely survived a storm at sea; and I gathered my things and left in haste. I turned to gaze at Marmilion before entering the oak alley; and against the sky of that gray morning, against the driven clouds, the old house heaved and rattled like a thing in pain, like a broken engine, like a ruined heart.

IX

Lydia gave birth to a baby girl in the summer of 1871, on August 24 to be precise; three days later she died. The delivery was long and painful. Dr. de Trot had no chloroform with which to ease the mother's ordeal; nor, one suspects, was he as scrupulous as he could have been about the complete and antiseptic removal of the afterbirth. He was an old man now, and his medical training had been undertaken in the 1820s. In any event, Lydia became infected, and de Trot stood by helplessly as puerperal fever ran its implacable course. Toward the end she apparently began to scream for her dead lover, Simon Grampus Lamar, until the convulsions exhausted her; on several occasions she even saw him at the end of her bed, and rose from her pillow, and beckoned him to come close . . . until, as the doctor records, *"soul and body could remain together no longer, and she was transplanted to flourish in a more congenial soil."*

In the Old South the aftermath of a death was governed by ritual; both conduct at the death scene and reporting of the death itself reflected strict rules of decorum. Relatives gathered, last words were carefully recorded, and coffin and funeral were chosen to demonstrate the wealth and status of the deceased's family. That was in the Old South; this was Reconstruction. Lydia died at the center of the bizarre microcosm Marmilion had become, a small world of anguished and embittered individuals, and her funeral was humble indeed. Caesar built the coffin, and an Episcopalian minister rode out to conduct the ceremony. The procession consisted of William and Camille,

Caesar, and Oscar de Trot; the doctor's old nag drew the wagon; and poor Lydia went to her rest beneath a simple wooden cross behind the disused sugar mill in the field beyond the kitchen garden. Her death did nothing to allay the animosity that crackled almost palpably now between the two men in the house—rather, the reverse, for William held Caesar directly responsible for the loss of his sister.

And now the story of Marmilion begins to move toward its grim, inexorable climax. Lydia's child was christened Emily, and Camille cared for her while Caesar labored in the garden. Almost single-handedly that silent man had brought forth fruit and vegetables from the wilderness Marmilion had been at the end of the war. There were pigs now, and chickens, and a cow; and he planned soon to replant the good field beyond the sugar mill with cane. Perhaps in the closeness of his heart Caesar entertained a vision of Marmilion returned to its former glory—with himself as master. Perhaps he even shared that vision with Camille. The old doctor gives us a picture of the household in this, its last period before the tragedy, with Caesar the devoted father returning each evening from the fields to gaze with mute adoration on the coffee-colored baby Camille tended as if she were her own; while upstairs, soaking in the venom secreted by his own vile heart, William Belvedere bitterly schemed the black man's destruction. We sometimes forget that the Creole aristocracy was descended from thieves, prostitutes, and lunatics—Parisian scum forcibly recruited to populate the colony in the reign of Louis XIV. We are about to witness the spectacle of one such aristocrat reverting to type.

X

(May 17, 1872)

The night was no worse than usual. I rose at eight o'clock and read two chapters in Hebrew and some Greek in Thucydides. I said my prayers and ate cake and boiled milk for breakfast. The weather was warm and sunny. I read a sermon and then took a little nap. I ate cowpeas and grits for dinner. In the afternoon I sat upon the necessary chair with scant result. I sat then upon my verandah and read a little Latin. Shortly before five o'clock I saw Caesar the Negroe coming across the fields. He walked like a sleeping man. He carried in his arms a bloody sheet that draped a corpse, and upon his back the swaddled form of his infant daughter. He entered my house without a word, and laid his burden on my table. I was forced to drive off the flies that clustered about it. It was with an exclamation of the deepest sorrow that I lifted the sheet and recognized thereunder the lifeless clay of the mistress of Marmilion. She had been dead some days. The Negroe gazed silently at his mistress for many minutes and though I ardently questioned him as to the circumstances of the tragedy he made no answer. Soon after he left my house, and I was unable to prevent his going. He made off toward the river. God help us all.

Despite the extensive searches that were mounted in the days that followed, Caesar and Emily were never found. Perhaps they got clear away, and started a new life in the North. Perhaps they were swallowed by the Mississippi.

XI

I have no more documentary evidence to offer. What follows is the construction of a sympathetic imagination.

It began, three days earlier, in the big room at the front of the house. Caesar was working there. He was sweeping out the ashes of last night's fire; or more probably—almost certainly—and this is a leap of the purest intuition—he was working with mortar and trowel, rebuilding the great pillar by the fireplace. William entered from the gallery with the shotgun. He stood in the doorway, and as Caesar went about his work he began to taunt him. I need not go into the precise character of his taunts; white men have been insulting black men in a manner essentially unchanged, I would guess, since—when?—Prince Henry's African expeditions? The wars between Rome and Carthage? The neolithic revolution of 1250 B.C.? William Belvedere stood taunting Caesar with a shotgun in the crook of his arm.

Caesar ignored him. William grew excited. Caesar at last rose to his feet, and turned toward his persecutor. It was at this moment that Camille, who had heard William's cries from upstairs, entered from the hallway. She saw her son pointing the shotgun at Caesar; and she saw Caesar standing by the broken pillar, a big man, physically strong, and unintimidated.

"Caesar!" she cried.

This is decisive. This is of crucial importance. For you see, Camille had not cried out to William to desist, to put aside the weapon; she had, instead, seen Caesar as the dangerous man, the dominant man; she had cried out to Caesar to back down, not William—and to that weak, contemptible creature this was the deepest cut of all: that even as he apparently held all the power in the situation, standing under his own roof with a shotgun pointing at a *slave,* his mother called upon the other to back down.

They both, Camille and Caesar, must have realized her mistake. Caesar stepped forward to take the gun from William; Camille darted between the two men; William, with his eyes closed, fired at his black nemesis—and his mother fell dead at his feet.

Oh, there is irony here, tragic irony; but what happened next? This is a mystery, for William, like his father, like Caesar and Emily, disappeared. They found bloodstains by the fireplace, and a discharged shotgun leaned against the wall. But they never found William.

Randolph Belvedere, in the opinion of Oscar de Trot, was killed in a duel. But what happened to William? I will tell you my conjecture. Consider: Caesar was a black nemesis, an agent of retributive justice; and he saw before him a vicious, despicable wretch, a wretch who stood for all the misery and oppression suffered by his race. That vile creature had just killed his, Caesar's, only friend and ally; and with her had died his dream of restoring Marmilion to its former glory—with himself as master! Oh, Caesar punished William, of this I have not the slightest doubt, for I've had a son of my own. And he made him suffer terribly, I have no doubt of that, either. And he made certain that no one would find him, that the blood-hounds and Klansmen that took up the chase would find no trace of William Belvedere. And William's spirit would know no rest, this was Caesar's intention; never would he lie in the soil with his sister, never would his spirit find peace. No, William's spirit would be trapped, it would be bricked up, to howl in endless torture in some prison of Caesar's construction—and there, close at hand, lay the tools to do it with! This was my conjecture—that Caesar bricked him up in that pillar by the fireplace, buried him alive, upright and conscious!

Maybe he chained him up in the pillar first, so that William could watch every single brick being fitted into its allotted place. God knows, there were enough chains, and shackles, and manacles, all the grim hard-ware of slavery, in Marmilion to enchain an army. Or possibly he drugged him first, so that when William emerged from an opiated daze he found himself sealed up tight in his tomb. I am certain he did not kill him first. William died slowly. He deserved to.

And it took three days for the plaster to dry. I am not a superstitious woman, but this was my conjecture. I'd heard him in there, you see.

XII

The last time I saw Marmilion I came in broad daylight; and as I emerged from the dappled shade of the oak alley, what a quiet glory the old house offered to my eye! The walls were of faded lemon-yellow, and where the plaster had crumbled the exposed brickwork was a beautiful soft red into which, in places, had seeped the grayness of moss. The window shutters and the railings of the galleries were a pale, weathered green; but loveliest of all was the woodwork of the entablature atop the pillars, which had been painted first sky-blue, then pink, then given a final wash of lavender such that it flushed in the sunshine with a delicate, roseate glow. No stone or metal, I now noticed, had been used in the construction of the house; entirely built of brick and timber, and lately touched by the encroaching vegetation, it rose from the soil, so it seemed, organically; and I was awed that despite the heat and damp of the semitropical climate, despite the ravages of neglect, and looting, and war, it yet retained in its decadence such dignity and strength.

I entered. The years had been less kind to Marmilion's interior. No line was straight; everything sagged and crumbled, and the walls were scabrous with mold, for the rainfall had loosened both plaster and woodwork. I realized, as I picked my way through the ruined rooms, that only the brickwork had resisted the damp. The two great chimneys rose through the structure like a pair of stanchions, or spines.

There were twenty-eight pillars girdling Marmilion, Corinthian pillars with fluted columns of plastered brick and elaborate, leafy capitals. The interior pillars echoed the design, even to the acanthus-leaf motif on the capitals. They were beautiful objects; it was a shame to destroy even one of them.

It was a day's work with crowbar and hammer to hack and claw that pillar by the fireplace to pieces. But finally I did it, and I found my skeleton. It was beautifully preserved, with not a bone out of place; it was delicate, fragile, white as china; but it was not the skeleton of William Belvedere. Perhaps, once again, I'd exercised too much sympathetic imagination. You see, what I'd found was the tiny, perfect skeleton—of a spider monkey.

Hand of a Wanker

ENTANKED IN THE ILL-LIT MOOD LOUNGE OF AN EAST
Village nightclub called Babylonia, a sleek green lizard with a crest of fine spines and a bright ruff under
its throat gazed unblinking into the glassy eyes of Lily
de Villiers. Lily peered back and tapped the tank with
a talonlike fingernail. On the couch beneath the video
screen Dicky Dee languidly eyed young Gunther, who
wore only purple lederhosen and had a magnificent
physique. Dicky himself was in plastic sandals, khaki
shorts, Hawaiian shirt, and white pith helmet.

"Lily," he murmured.

The lizard didn't move, and nor did Lily.

"Lily."

"Oh, what?"

"Fix me a drink, sweetie."

It was late afternoon, the club was empty, and the

bar was open. Lily straightened up and wobbled over on heels like needles. As she reached for the vodka, Dicky's eyes wandered back to young Gunther's pectorals. Upstairs a telephone rang. The air conditioner was humming. It was summer, and no one was in town. Then Lily screamed.

"Oh, good God, what is it?" exclaimed Dicky.

Lily was staring at something in the sink. She picked it up gingerly, then screamed again and flung it on the bar.

"It's real!" she cried.

"What is?" said Dicky, gazing at the ceiling.

"It's a—hand!"

A faint gleam appeared in Dicky Dee's eyes. "A hand?" he murmured, rising from the couch.

THE MOOD LOUNGE WAS A LONG ROOM WITH A LOW CEILing and no windows. The bar occupied one end and there was a stuffed ostrich at the other. A few tables and chairs were scattered about the floor. In the permanent gloom one did not notice that the paint was peeling and the linoleum cracking; for usually the place was full of decadent types gossiping in blasé tones about drugs, love, and disease. But this was the afternoon; it was summertime; and they were the only ones in there.

Dicky peered at the thing on the bar. It was indeed a hand. The skin was pale, with fine black hairs on the back and, oddly enough, the palm. The blood on the stump was black, and congealed, though the fingernails were nicely trimmed. Dicky looked from Lily to Gunther and back to the hand. Tittering slightly, he took the cigarette from his mouth and put it between the fingers.

"Oh, Dicky!" cried Lily, turning away. "How could you? It might be someone we know."

"True," said Dicky, taking back his cigarette. "Anyway, you need a lung to smoke. Let's go and tell Yvonne. Maybe it's Yvonne's hand."

YVONNE WAS IN CHARGE OF BOOKINGS, AND COULD BE found in the office at this time of day. When Lily and Dicky came in, he was peering anxiously at a calendar covered with illegible scrawls and mumbling into a phone squashed between ear and shoulder. They could see immediately that both his hands were firmly attached to their wrists. He raised his eyes toward the ceiling, pressed his lips together, and pulled his mouth into a long sagging line of weary resignation. With his off-white mohawk tumbling in disarray about his ears, he looked, thought Dicky, rather like a sheep.

"I'm going to put you on hold, Tony," he said. "Something's come up." He hung up.

"Come downstairs, darling," said Dicky Dee. "You need a drink." Yvonne glanced at Lily's face. Why was the girl so pale? It was rather becoming. He rose from his desk like a man in pain and ran a thin bejeweled hand through his hair. "I think I do," he said. Down they went then, Yvonne and Dicky in front, and Lily tottering behind them.

*   *   *

BUT WHEN THEY GOT TO THE LOUNGE, THE HAND WAS gone.

"It's gone!" cried Dicky.

"What?" said Yvonne.

"There was a severed hand on the bar!"

Yvonne sighed, and began to make himself a drink. Dicky Dee turned to young Gunther, who was still sitting on the couch and still flexing his pecs.

"Gunther, what happened to the hand?" Dicky appeared rattled. He generated emotion.

Gunther shrugged.

"Hands don't just—disappear!" whispered Dicky, blanching.

Yvonne shrugged. Gunther shrugged again. Lily was looking under the bar, joggling the bottles. "Maybe it slipped down," she said. Then she screamed—for out of the darkness leaped the hand itself!

It scampered across the bar, hurled itself onto the floor, then scuttled down the room and out the door at the end. There was a moment of stunned silence, and then Yvonne dropped his drink. It shattered messily on the floor.

"Mein Gott," breathed Gunther. "The dead hand lives."

Dicky strode manfully toward the door. "I'm going after it," he said. Then he stopped, turned, and came back to the bar. "I think I need a little drink first," he said. "This is extremely fucking weird."

NONE OF THEM MENTIONED WHAT THEY'D SEEN. THEY sensed, rightly, that others would be skeptical; the staff of Babylonia had never been known for rigor in perceptual matters. Three nights later, Saint Mark and his Evangelists were playing the upstairs room. Toward the end of their late set, Saint Mark paused to catch his breath and introduce the next "song."

"This one's called 'Witch-Bitch,' " he grunted, fingering his iron cross. "Dedicated to my mother—"

Then he screamed.

The audience thought the scream was all part of it. The band knew it wasn't, and so did Dicky Dee. He'd seen the hand dropping from the ceiling, and he rushed for the stage as Saint Mark staggered backwards into the drums, clawing at the thing clamped to his neck. The kids applauded with gusto as the skinny singer overturned a cymbal, and by the time Dicky got onstage the rest of the band was desperately attempting to pry the hand off Saint Mark's neck. But the diabolical fingers could not be moved. Saint Mark's face, meanwhile, had turned scarlet, his eyes were bulging grotesquely, and his tongue protruded thickly from his throat. The applause had by this time turned to a hubbub of confusion and horror, but through it all Dicky could hear one clear voice:

"Burn it off! Burn it off!"

Of course! Dicky Dee lit a cigarette with trembling fingers and ground it into the back of the hand. It was a dramatically effective move. The hand immediately loosed its grip and scuttled under an upset drum—and not a moment too soon, as far as Saint Mark was concerned. They helped him offstage, and by a stroke of good fortune there were stimulants on hand to help revive the half-choked performer. He was soon his old "self" again, apparently none the worse for his encounter with the hand.

"But where did it come from?" he said, gently fingering his long white stringy neck. No one could answer him. "What a grip," he said, in a tone of some respect. "Look at those bruises!" They looked at the bruises; and within an hour, a number of leading Babylonians were sporting on their necks cosmetic stranglemarks in exquisitely brutal shades of red, purple, and black.

THREE DAYS LATER LILY WAS TENDING BAR UPSTAIRS when she noticed a rather unusual character enter the club. He stood close to the door, grinning wildly at nothing in particular as his eyes darted suspiciously from side to side. But what struck Lily as odd was this: when he paid for his Guinness, and she caught a glimpse of his palm—there were hairs growing on it! She was about to strike up a conversation on the topic when the tranquility of Babylonia was yet again shattered by a hideous scream. It came from the ladies' washroom—and a moment later a young woman came crashing through the door, still pulling up her fishnet tights.

"Fucking men!" she shouted. "You can't take a piss without being molested!" She collapsed onto a barstool, and to the small crowd of anxious drinkers that quickly gathered round she pointed with trembling finger into the washroom. "In there!" she cried.

"What, a man?" said Lily. It had happened before.

"No!" wailed the distressed girl. "A man's *hand!*"

Lily looked at Dicky, who had just emerged from the office, and Dicky dashed into the washroom. A moment later he came out again. "It's gone," he said.

"Back where it came from, I hope!" said the girl, with a shudder of deep distaste.

THE STORY, AS DICKY AND LILY TOLD IT TO YVONNE in the office a few minutes later, was that the hand had been lurking in the U-bend of the toilet upon which the unfortunate girl had seated herself, and the temptation, clearly, had been irresistible. When the girl had fled, shrieking, the hand had in all probability returned to the safety of the U-bend.

"So at least we know it's amphibious," murmured Yvonne.

"It's amphibious, cunning, murderous—and horny," said Dicky, pacing back and forth. "The question is—"

At that moment there was a loud rap at the door. "Go away!" shouted Yvonne.

There was a moment's silence; then the rap came again.

"Go away!" shouted Yvonne and Lily. But the door opened, and there stood the black-clad stranger whom Lily had noticed earlier—the one with hair on the palm of his hand!

"Excuse me," he said in deep, hollow tones.

Yvonne rose irritably to his feet. "We're in a meeting," he grumbled. "Can't you—"

"The hand," said the stranger. "I can help you."

Yvonne stopped in his tracks. "You can?" he said. "What do you know?"

"May I come in?" said the stranger.

"Come in, come in," said Yvonne, pushing a chair forward. "Tell us what you know."

"Very well," said the stranger, seating himself and pulling a cigarette from his pocket. "Mind if I smoke?"

"Smoke, smoke," said Yvonne. "Just tell us about the hand."

So the stranger told them about the hand.

THE CURSE OF HUMAN DESIRE

The stranger accepted a light from Yvonne, drew heavily on his cigarette, and stared at the floor. At last he lifted his eyes—tormented, bloodshot eyes, filmed with despair—and Lily felt a small gush of pity for the man. There were deep bags under his eyes, and his skin was unnaturally pale. "You see before you," he said at last, in those hollow tones of his, "a victim of human desire. Not a pretty sight, is it?" There was another pause. Yvonne cleared his voice and said: "Who—"

"Oh, my name doesn't matter," said the stranger. "I am just one of many, a ruined man, ruined by . . ." Here he was unable to finish his sentence; a sob racked his frame.

"Human desire?" said Dicky.

"Exactly!" said the stranger. "Everywhere I look I see lips, breasts, bottoms, legs—and I've had enough! I can't stand it anymore—this constant itch—this *compulsion!* I'm a sick man!" he cried—and then his voice dropped an octave, or more. "I'm a compulsive masturbator, you see," he whispered. "I have to wank. And this"—he slowly opened his hand—"is the result." It was then that Dicky and Yvonne saw what

Lily had seen earlier: dead in the center of his palm sprouted a small clump of fine black hairs.

"Just like an armpit," murmured Yvonne. "Go on."

"It all began," continued the stranger, "with the onset of puberty. Slowly it took over my life. I couldn't escape; it was like a machine, constantly filling my head with these—images!" He shuddered. "I lost my job. Dishonorable discharge. Ha! Story of my life. . . ." There was a long silence. Then, lifting his eyes, the stranger said quietly: "How long can a man live with shame?"

Dicky looked at Yvonne. Yvonne shrugged. "We don't know," he said. "How long?"

"Only so long!" the stranger cried, and suddenly rising to his feet, he pulled from his pocket, where it had been tucked since the beginning of the interview, his right hand—only there was no right hand! He hauled up his sleeve to show how the wrist ended in a smooth, round, dimpled stump. Wordlessly the three Babylonians gazed at the stranger's stump. They'd not met a story like this one before, and Lily slipped out to get them all a drink.

"You can still do it with your left one, I suppose?" said Yvonne.

"Masturbation guilt drove me to it," said the stranger, resuming his seat. "Yes, masturbation guilt! I hacked it off myself, and I should have drowned it, I suppose, but I couldn't bring myself to do it. . . ." There was a pregnant silence. "I come from a sentimental race, you see," he went on. "I put it in a shoe box and kept it under the sink instead."

"A shoe box," said Lily, who had returned with drinks. "Cute."

"Oh, there were holes in it," said the stranger, taking a long swallow of his Guinness. "But anyway, for a week I wasn't troubled by the curse of human desire—yes, for the first time since puberty I didn't feel the itch! Can you imagine it—a world without breasts, without skin, without bums and lips and legs . . . a world free of desire, where everything is what it seems and your brain isn't polluted with longing and your loins aren't constantly stirring with a life of their own . . . can you imagine what it is to be free of human desire?"

They all nodded.

"It couldn't last. It returned in the depths of the night, as I slept. I felt it creep under the blankets. I felt its fingers on my thigh, soft as silk. I felt it gently laying hold of me—and I rose up from my bed with a shout and I *hurled* the thing from me! Oh, I couldn't have it starting again, not after all I'd been through! 'Back to your box!' I shouted; and to see it drag itself out the door and into the kitchen—it was a pathetic sight, so it was. But I had to be firm, you see that?"

They all nodded.

"I never saw it again," said the stranger. There was a long pause. A muted roar of conversation was audible from the bar beyond. At last Dicky spoke. "And you think it's your hand that's been causing the trouble here?" he said.

"I do," said the stranger, who had finished his Guinness and pulled out another cigarette. "I was in here the night before—before I cut it off. I think it remembers. I think it came back." He clutched his face in his hand. "Oh, God," he sobbed, "if only I'd been strong. If only I'd flushed it down the toilet in the beginning—"

"It wouldn't have done any good," Dicky cut in. "It's amphibious."

"No!" said the stranger.

"But more to the point," said Dicky, "how can we catch it?"

"Oh, I'll tell you how to catch it," said the stranger. "And I'll tell you what to do with it once you've caught it." And he pulled from inside his coat a hefty meat cleaver—the very same one, he told them, he'd used on the hand in the first place. And then he outlined his plan. . . .

DER TOD UND DIE HAND

Late that night—very late, when the club had emptied and everyone had gone home to bed—or to the after-hours place on Avenue B—Lily de Villiers sat alone in the ill-lit mood lounge of Babylonia. She was looking her best. Her red hair was piled up on top, with thick strands curling saucily down around her face and throat. Her eyes were heavily mascaraed, and her lips were scarlet. Rouge highlights on her cheeks created an impression of mounting inner passion. She was in deep décolletage, her cleavage shadow sharply accentuated by the subdued lighting of the mood lounge, and her little leather skirt riding high up thighs sheathed in black seamed nylon stockings with runs and ladders and other tarty insignia. Her legs were crossed and her heels, as ever, were like needles. She was heavily

178

perfumed. She exuded availability. She was the whore of Babylonia, and she was there to bait the hand.

An hour passed, and Lily sat smoking cigarettes and pouting provocatively. She crossed and recrossed her legs every few minutes, and the ashtray on the couch beside her gradually filled. Lily got to her feet and, unsure what strange eye might be watching, tottered sexily over to the bar and emptied the ashtray into a garbage can. Then she returned to the couch and resumed sitting, smoking, pouting, waiting, and crossing and recrossing her legs.

Another hour passed. Poor Lily was starting to yawn. The sun was coming up. Honest citizens were going to work. She was about to call it a night and go upstairs to the others when a tiny sound caught her attention. Could it be? It could; someone—or something—was coming down the stairs!

Lily smoked with a careless nonchalance honed to perfection by years of practice. She was very cool. And there it was!—pattering across the floor like a hideous pink crab, slapping the linoleum as it scampered toward her in lusty and intemperate haste. From fifteen feet it hurled itself upon her, groping like a maniac at her bosom! Lily rose into the air with a wild shriek of horror, then toppled backwards as from beneath the couch reared young Gunther, who had been waiting there all the while, and who now brandished aloft the stranger's meat cleaver! Lily seized the hand and plucked it from her bosom like a limpet from a rock and hurled it with a cry of disgust against the wall. The hand fell, stunned, to the floor, and lay on its back, its white, tender, hairy underside exposed to the fierce lunge of the young German. Then down came the cleaver and mercilessly hacked the dazed hand in two! The shattered and bleeding half-hands lurched off in opposite directions, but far too shakily to escape Gunther's terrible wrath. Slash slash! Down came the cleaver twice more, and the hand was severed in four. From four to eight and from eight to sixteen; and when the cursed creature that had spilled the stranger's seed so needlessly all those years was finally reduced to somewhere in the region of fifty parts, and none of them was moving, Gunther stopped. He mopped his brow and lifted his head, his breast damp and heaving, to the light, which Dicky Dee had just flicked on.

"Good work, Gunther," said Dicky, his eyes burning with a morbid and unnatural gleam. "And Lily"—he went to the poor girl, who was rising unsteadily to her feet after gazing aghast at Gunther's grunty choppings; "my poor dear Lily. A hero!"

"Heroine," gasped Lily.

"Heroine!" cried Dicky.

"Heroine," murmured Yvonne, entering.

"Heroine!" thundered Gunther, brandishing the bloody cleaver.

At that moment the stranger's hollow tones were heard. "The hand is dead," he said, from the doorway at the top of the stairs. "Feed it to the lizard. Long live the hand!" And with a dry, bitter laugh—or was it just a bad cough, a dirty hack spawned of some putrid existential miasma that seethed within his guilt-ridden soul?—anyway, with a sound that chilled the racing, roaring blood of the four young people, the stranger waved his stump over his head and limped off into the sharp Manhattan dawn.

The Boot's Tale

I AM, IT IS TRUE, A MERE BOOT, AND NO LONGER YOUNG. My leather is wrinkled now, soft to the touch, and circumstance has shaped me to its whims. My sole flaps; my grommets, those that remain, are rusty; and I no longer gleam in the sunshine as I did before the war. In those days I was a working boot, and no stranger to turf, and soil, and the gravel of suburban driveways; and though I am old and stiff now, I still dream of once more lacing tightly to a healthy ankle and treading the mulch of a green and fertile earth.

A mere boot. Nevertheless, I speak, that those of you who come after—if such there be—may profit in wisdom from what I am about to impart. My service was not elevated, but I worked diligently for the old order, and would see its return. I stand to gain nothing from distorting the truth.

There were four of them to begin with. Gerty Murgatroid was the matriarch, a pale, fat woman who sat out her days with a bowl of junk food in the valley between her thighs and an unending dirge of negativity on her thin gill-like lips. Her eyes were like a fish's, fixed and glassy, squeezed between lardy wedges of white fat whence they gazed constant and unblinking at a television screen. Her little bulb of a head was tufted with a few wisps of dry, fluffy hair, and it wobbled continually atop its vast immobile housing of flesh. In a faded housedress and defeated slippers Gerty endured the empty days; and her husband, Herb, a small, neat, compulsive man with bitten fingernails and a pencil-thin mustache, tinkered away in the den with his "projects," and when forced to interact with his wife was unable to control a tic that flickered violently at the corner of his left eye and contorted his expression into a hideous rictus to which strangers reacted with horror but which Gerty herself had long since accepted as a manifestation of Herb's "nerves."

To tread again the mulch of a green and fertile earth. . . . There is no green and fertile earth, not now. Your earth is cold now, strewn with rubble and dead things, and upon it lies an unmelting blanket of black snow. For months there was only night, as the sunlight which shone once upon my buffed and vaulted toecap was blocked by a great grimy veil of smoke and lofted soot, and the snow that fell was black. I survived that terrible winter; I went into the shelter with the canned goods and the blankets and the paperbacks and the tranquilizers, and was tossed into a corner. In the weeks that followed I observed the decline and fall of an American family.

*   *   *

HERB AND GERTY'S RELATIONSHIP COULD NOT BE CALLED a loving one; and yet they managed to develop a habit of coexistence that permitted each to function according to his or her bent, and in this way they were not unlike a pair of boots, as I often remarked to my own mate and colleague, a trusty bit of footwear boiled, alas, in a soup in the days of famine that followed the war.

There were two children: Ann, a silent and delicate girl who took after her father; and fat Peter, an endomorph like Gerty. Fat Peter was a smelly, freckled boy with dirty hair and a grimy T-shirt that strained vainly to contain the jellied bulk of his tummy. A merry lad, he liked to tear the wings off houseflies and pepper the eyes of dogs. He put frogs in bottles and gleefully hurled them skywards, and small creatures scattered at his approach. His schoolmates, whom he bullied, avoided him like the plague, for to fat Peter all of Nature was a victim to be terrorized and mutilated without mercy. And thus did he discharge the pain of parental neglect, for Herb and Gerty, devoid of emotion themselves, were oblivious to the needs of their children.

But not oblivious to the impending catastrophe of Western Civilization. A plumber by trade, and a paranoid by nature, Herb had been painstakingly converting the basement into a long-term fallout shelter; and as luck would have it, on the very day he finished the job—it was a Sunday afternoon in late September— the fateful announcement was made. Gerty heard it first, and her voice sliced through the house like a carving knife.

"Herb!" she screeched. "Get up here!"

I was on the back porch at the time, enjoying the unseasonable sunshine. I counted slowly to seven; this pause permitted Herb to murmur a string of unspeakable blasphemies under his breath, and the tic in his face to start twitching. The familiar patter up the basement stairs; then, "Yes, dear?"

"Turn it up! Turn it up!"

". . . we repeat," said the TV, "reports are coming in that the Eastern Seaboard has been devastated by a missile strike. The President has ordered massive retaliation, and urges the American people to go calmly to their shelters and remain there until further notice. This has been a recording. We repeat . . ."

"It's war!" shrieked Gerty. "Do something!"

It often takes a crisis to bring out the best in a man, and when Herb Murgatroid spoke again, there was a note of authority in his voice I had never heard there before.

"Go downstairs, Gerty," he said firmly. "Take Ann. I'll fetch Peter."

There was a moment of silence; then Gerty assented, and could be heard heaving ponderously up out of her armchair, and shouting for her daughter. A few seconds later I was on Herb's foot and running toward the playground where fat Peter was whiling away his afternoon. All down the street doors were opening and troubled citizens emerging to gather in small knots and gaze at the sky. We found fat Peter surrounded by a gang of little children, to whom he was demonstrating the correct method of eviscerating a bat. Herb laid a hand on his son's plump shoulder.

"Come home now, Peter," he said. "There's an emergency."

"Not now, Pop," grinned the obese child, his fingers dripping with bat entrails, "I wanna—"

"Now, Peter!" barked Herb. The small children fell back, startled. Other parents breathlessly arrived to drag off their offspring. Whining all the way, fat Peter was marched home under the uncharacteristically firm hand of his father, and down into the family fallout shelter. And so it began.

HERB, BEING A PLUMBER, HAD SEEN TO ALL THE LIFE-support systems necessary to maintain the family underground for the duration. Odd, then, that he had not factored in the psychic strains that were bound to arise—for the nuclear family is very much like a hydraulic machine, and unless it's adequately equipped with safety valves, pressure within the closed system may rise to dangerous levels. After a couple of weeks fat Peter, who had victimized the weak for most of his young life, found himself the target of collective family tension. Not only was he the youngest, he was also now the loudest; for his mother suffered a profound shock when the television networks closed down, and lapsed into a quasicatatonic stupor from which she would never be aroused. So fat Peter was unconsciously selected to absorb the psychological toxins generated in the desperate confines of the Murgatroid bunker, and his wheezy laughter was soon replaced by a dark and brooding sullenness.

Herb's assertiveness, meanwhile, increased in inverse proportion to Gerty's collapse: he waxed as she waned, and thus was homeostasis preserved. However, he was pretty shaken when he learned that the heavy pall of radiation drifting overhead was a good deal more dense and slow-moving than he'd been led to expect. And with the realization that the family would have to spend a considerable period of time underground, Herb decided that rationing must be immediately introduced.

He made his announcement at the next family meal. Gerty, her mind now rarely active and her body increasingly inert, did not heed the message. Ann looked anxiously at her father, but said nothing. Fat Peter began to whine.

"Hey, Pop, I'm sick of eating stuff out of cans. Ain't there any real food, Pop; ain't there any *meat?*"

"No meat," snapped Herb. "Only canned food now, and less of it. It may be months before we can leave."

"Months? Hey, Pop, it ain't so bad up there; can't we try it for a while? I wanna go to the store."

"Shut up, Peter," said Ann. "Daddy knows what he's talking about. He's got instruments."

Peter rounded furiously on his sister. "Blow it out your ass, shitface!" he yelled. "I want some meat!"

"Peter!" bellowed Herb, rising to his feet and pointing to the back of the shelter. "Go to your room. Now!"

"I want some meat," whimpered the fat, unhappy boy. "I hate this canned garbage."

"Go to your room, Peter," repeated Herb, his pointing finger aquiver with mounting anger.

"Yes, Peter," said Ann. "Go to your room like Daddy says."

Fat Peter started up, the tears cutting wide channels down his plump and dirty cheeks. The cold eyes of his father and sister gazed at him with implacable distaste.

Gerty had already returned to her armchair, and slumped into the sleep that claimed her now for twenty hours out of the twenty-four. The weeping boy ran to his mother, and threw himself upon her gently heaving bosom; then he fumbled at her housecoat buttons, glancing furtively over his shoulder at the others. Suddenly he parted his mother's garment and bared a vast milkwhite breast. Ann's hands flew to her mouth and she turned wide-eyed to her father. Herb was still on his feet, still pointing, and speechless with rage. Fat Peter had meanwhile buried his face in his mother's breast and was sucking lustily at a large purplish nipple. Herb strode across the room and, pulling his belt out of his trousers, lashed his son's back. A muffled scream issued from deep within the wobbling lake of flesh that was Gerty Murgatroid's breast, but the great mother did not awaken, nor did fat Peter loosen his grip upon her. Herb, livid with fury, lashed again, and this time the boy's head came up. Herb grabbed him by the scruff of the neck and dragged him off his wife.

"Go to your room," he commanded. "Now!"

Fat Peter was squirming on the floor of the bomb shelter, shielding his face from his father's belt. "I'm hungry," he wailed in his distress. "I'm hungry."

"To—your—room," ordered his father again, and blinded by his own tears, the boy crawled off on his hands and knees, Herb following right behind. Ann had by this time recovered from her shock, and darted across the room to cover her mother's bosom and rebutton the housedress. Then she returned to the table; and Gerty slept on, oblivious.

*   *   *

FOUR DAYS LATER GERTY WAS AGAIN SLEEPING AND Herb was at his instruments when fat Peter and Ann heard a scraping noise at the top of the basement steps. The two children looked at each other. "I'm going to tell Daddy," said Ann.

"Wait," said fat Peter. In silent suspense they waited; and then came the scrape again. Fat Peter motioned to Ann to come with him, and the pair ascended the stairs till their ears were pressed against the thick, bolted, insulated door.

"Who is it?" said fat Peter.

"Let us in," came a feeble voice. "We're starving . . . we're freezing . . . let us in."

Now, fat Peter and Ann were too young to know it, but they were in fact caught in one of the knottier ethical dilemmas of the postapocalyptic era. It was the nuclear lifeboat question: does one hoard resources for one's own family and turn away the needy stranger, to almost certain death; or does one share with the needy stranger, thereby reducing one's own stocks and jeopardizing the family? It's a meaty question, but fat Peter unfortunately did not have the moral equipment to do it justice.

"Fuck off!" he shouted, and began to giggle for the first time in weeks. His mirth was contagious.

"Fuck off!" shouted Ann. "There's only enough for the Murgatroids!"

"Only enough for the Murgatroids!" screamed fat Peter, dissolving into fresh gales of laughter and help-lessly wetting his pants.

"Let us in," came the voice, fainter still. "We're starving."

188

"Only enough for the Murgatroids! Only enough for the Murgatroids!"

When Herb at last appeared, and asked what all the noise was about, Ann brought herself under control and told him. He frowned a moment, his tic flicked once, and then he said, "That's right, only enough for the Murgatroids"—and returned to his instruments.

GERTY PASSED AWAY ABOUT A MONTH LATER. SHE SUDdenly sat bolt upright in her armchair, her eyes wide open; up came a thick string of bloody sputum, and then she fell back stone dead on the cushions. No one was particularly distraught, and she was laid out on the floor, under a sheet, while Herb figured out what to do with the corpse. Next day he had his answer.

It was breakfast time, and the two children were silently pushing baked beans about their plates. Herb appeared at the head of the table and gazed sternly at them.

"Answer me truthfully," he said in a very grave voice. "Who took one of Mommy's fingers during the night?"

Ann emitted a small scream and covered her mouth with her hands. Fat Peter turned a deep scarlet and started to bluster.

"I don't know, Pop. Finger, what finger? Who, me?"

"Don't lie to me, Peter," roared his father. "Bring me the remains!"

Fat Peter, without another word, left the breakfast table and padded off to his bedroom. A moment later he reappeared and, flinching slightly, held out to his father a well-gnawed fingerbone. "I was hungry," he said weakly.

"Peter!" breathed Ann.

Herb looked strangely at his son. "Didn't you," he finally said, "even try to *cook* it?"

Fat Peter shrugged, and stared at his shoes—a friendly pair of cheap Korean runners who bore the immense strain of the boy's extremities with uncomplaining stoicism. Then he looked up again, clearly puzzled—as were we all—that Herb had not flown into a rage. His tic wasn't even flickering. Instead, he was still gazing curiously at fat Peter who, it was now clear, had bloodstains on the front of his T-shirt. "Come with me, Ann," he said; "I have something to explain to you. You stay here, Peter."

Half-an-hour later Herb and fat Peter had laid a plastic sheet on the floor of the bomb shelter and stretched dead Gerty out on it, stark naked and face down. Then Herb took up his carving knife and sliced a few good rashers off one of his wife's great buttocks, and set them carefully on a sheet of greaseproof paper. Fat Peter grinned at his dad and licked his lips.

"Not yet, Peter," said Herb. "We have work to do."

In the hours that followed I was forced to make serious adjustments to the high opinion I had thus far formed of your people. Of course I understood Herb Murgatroid's thinking: the family was running out of food and Gerty had to be disposed of; these were apocalyptic times and conventional moral norms had lost all relevance; the family was cut off and therefore unlikely to infect the social body by its transgression; and so on. But even so, something galled me about the haste and ease with which the venerable taboo was violated. There was no sense of awe, no mystery, nothing of the sublime, and this I regretted. It seems to me that if you're going to eat each other, there should at least be ritual, for anthropophagy, when all is said and done, is still a rather grand and dignified sin. It *matters*. I'm only a boot, of course, but Herb and fat Peter went about it as if—as if they were working in a fast-food joint. And most of the footwear in the fallout shelter were with me on this: it was a crude and vulgar display, and we all agreed that a European family would have handled things much more tastefully.

But I digress. In the hours that followed, Gerty Murgatroid was butchered, and her various limbs and organs carefully wrapped and deposited in the freezer, which had of course long since been emptied. And when the bloody job was over, and everything had been cleaned up, the two hungry males minced some buttock and fried it up in patties and devoured it with relish; and for the first time in many, many weeks a ruddy glow returned to their faces, and father and son grinned at each other in the lamplight, and murmured that it was mighty tasty, and so on.

FINALLY THE BLACK CLOUDS OF NUCLEAR WINTER cleared, and Herb decided it was safe to go up. Since Gerty's death the family had eaten well, Ann having gotten over her qualms after a few days, and all were plump and rosy as they hauled on their coats and scarves and boots. I was, of course, a member of this expedition, and I was extremely curious to see what had happened to that green and fertile earth I'd once known.

And so we emerged. It was, as I've said, a cold, bleak, black and dreary wasteland of a world we found, and we were all very disturbed. The three Murgatroids stamped through the snow, checking over the ruins and kicking aside small piles of charred bones. The sun was rising into a deep brown sky, and to the west, where once had been a complex of shopping malls and superhighways, there glimmered a dead gray lake, with an occasional blackened girder poking up like the twisted limb of some great fallen giant. Up here on the high ground it was still dry; and then fat Peter saw something.

"Look, Pop!" he shouted. "A bonfire!"

It was, indeed, a bonfire, burning brightly in the skeleton of a ruined building about half a mile away; and there seemed to be some movement around it. It was many months since the Murgatroids had known society, and as they hastened across the wasteland one could detect arising in each of them a small flame of hope. They entered the crumbling shell and made their way toward the bonfire, but as they did so the survivors clustered close to the flames turned to them, and the family hesitated. For these people were stick-thin, white as chalk, their faces cratered with running sores and the eyes, deep in hollow and blackened sockets, almost completely extinguished. They'd been roasting rats on sticks, but on seeing the Murgatroids they began to draw back into the shadows; and it was not hard to understand why. To these starving and irradiated half-humans the plump and robust good health of the Murgatroids must have seemed monstrous, truly monstrous. And so would it to me, I reflected, as Herb and Ann and fat Peter edged cautiously forward, puzzled, and calling out greetings to the people who'd all now vanished. Good health and a well-fed belly would of course seem monstrous in a world of chronic and terminal hunger, a world where deprivation was the norm; and barely had I begun to see the Murgatroids as monsters when the stick-thin people emerged from the shadows and battered them to death with clubs, and feasted on them as they'd feasted on Gerty.

My mate, as I say, was boiled in a soup a few days later, but I was somehow overlooked. The stick-thin people will cling to life for a few more weeks, a month or two if they're lucky, and then they'll succumb to postnuclear conditions. It's a wonder they've lasted this long. I can still see a few Murgatroid bones here and there, protruding from the black snow and the ashes, and I wonder about the future. Sometimes I imagine a pair of small wings sprouting from my uppers, and I see myself flapping off, leaving all this behind, climbing through the clouds into the thin clear air, higher and higher, a tiny winged boot ascending to God.

The E(rot)ic Potato

I AM A FLY CALLED GILBERT AND I LIVE BY A POND, A stagnant pond in a bird sanctuary. The surface of the pond is covered by a carpet of tiny bright green organic discs. The reeds and the rushes still thrust up from the muddy bed below, and as the breeze plays over the water the leafy tendrils of a weeping willow on the bank stir gently. Climb the bank and you will find, set back in the trees, a tumbledown shed. This is where the E(ROT)IC POTATO is.

One day I flew up the bank where the shadows hang and the ivy claws at the gray stones edging flatly out of the irradiated earth. Forms of other insects flashed by me. I settled upon a branch and turned my compound eyes toward the shed which housed the E(ROT)IC POTATO. It lay beneath the trees, and though its windows were smashed and boarded up with cardboard, its roof was whole. The white paint was peeling off the boards, and the door was held closed by a rusty

194

nail. One hinge hung loose. The sharp tap of a bird's beak rattled suddenly through the air. A butterfly emerged from between the cardboard and the shattered windowpane. A rusting tool, half in sunlight and half in shadow, was leaned against the wall beside the shaky door. I did not go further. I knew I would be turned back. I was not yet ready to enter the presence of the E(ROT)IC POTATO. The emergent butterfly drifted by me in the dappled woodland sunlight, and I returned to the pond.

On the way I found a fairly large crowd of insects gathered round a poisoned water rat, and the air was abuzz with the vibrations of fine wings and the chatter of excited voices. The creature lay on the bank shivering, for its pelt had lost the sleek oily texture that insulates the mammal within. After a few feeble attempts to haul its body up the bank it collapsed limply and lay panting, near death, in the mud. A yellow fluid seeped thickly from its ears and eyes, and a greenish discoloration spread across its soft underbelly. As the breathing grew heavier, the mouth opened and sucked air and we saw that its teeth had crumbled to impotent stumps. A rat without teeth was doomed, in our world.

Several flies and some ants had already mounted the body and were sampling tissue. They quickly discovered that the irradiation was mild, and once again we were confronted by proof of our biological superiority: that rat couldn't breathe our air and live. A warm pulse ran through the crowd, and then we set to.

There was more than enough for all, but naturally we wanted to lay open the belly first and get at the inner organs. The biters and chewers were quickly ushered to the front, and went to work. The rest of us buzzed about, making inroads where we could. I was set to breaking down blockage in the left ear, to clear a passage to the brain.

Some time later word spread that the ants had got through, and we buzzed down to have a look. Ariadne the dragonfly had been flitting about the head for a while, and flew close to me on the short hop to the opened belly. I was thrilled by her proximity, and though our eyes did not meet I knew she was aware of me.

There was a buzzy crunch on the belly of the water rat, and in all the confusion of eager mandibles and flashing wings my body drew very close to Ariadne's. I felt a tremor run through her as my proboscis glanced against her articulated thorax, and then something rather wonderful happened. Ariadne fluttered aloft and, hovering close, delicately displayed the milkwhite tip of her ovipositor to me. I was flooded by an irresistible genetic impulse to penetrate and fertilize her, but the trembling organ was withdrawn and the flashing blue-green dragonfly fluttered away.

Then, before my reeling senses could recover, they were again bombarded, this time by a meaty waft of warm fresh mammalian intestine. At that point I lost control completely and plunged into the innards of the rat's body with my fellows and fed.

THE MEAL CONTINUED AS THE SUN MOVED ACROSS AN intensely brown sky. In the late afternoon, when the pond lay in shadow and nothing stirred the reeds, and the dripping tendrils of the weeping willow ululated imperceptibly and the tranquility was broken only by the endless declamations of the throstle-throated birds, and the countless tiny bright green organic discs had silently meshed to form an unbroken slimy weave over the poisoned water, the crab arrived.

"My turn, I think," he murmured as he eased his great plated frame sideways up the bank. There was a din of protest at this, but the crustacean could not have cared less for the shrill outrage of a fly. He thrust a massive claw into the cadaver; and then, in full view of the assembled insects, he scooped out and consumed a dripping, glistening mountain of our eggs! The uproar intensified, but with utter indifference the hoary old scavenger shuffled his cantankerous and exoskeletal self entirely inside the rat's body, and within a few moments a steady, muffled grumble, basso profundo, was all that could be heard. He emerged, some time later, eructating, and made his way sideways back to the pond.

THAT NIGHT ARIADNE ADMITTED ME TO THE E(ROT)IC POTATO. In a darkness strangely alive we flew from the body of the dead rat up the bank and through the trees to the shed. A full moon, tinted with toxins to the color of a rotting orange, bathed our rickety little temple in the febrile glow of postapocalyptic romance. Ariadne's articulated rear segment trailed through the moonbeams and I flew steadily in her wake, inhaling drunkenly the subtle wisplets of insect love juice she was secreting. She landed with grace upon the edge of the windowframe and I came down beside her a moment later, swooning foolishly, barely conscious.

There were wasps everywhere. They swarmed about the shattered windowframe and squeezed themselves between the shards and the cardboard in the moonlight. Ariadne, her long smooth gauzy wings folded perpendicular above herself, twitched her slender tail sharply as one of these guardians approached us. I knew enough to let her do the talking.

"Good evening," said the wasp smoothly.

Ariadne, rubbing her gossamer wings one against the other and filling the air with a silky rustle that excited me beyond words, graced the handsome big stinger with a dazzling multifaceted glance.

"Ariadne," said the wasp, with pleasure. "And—a small fly?" I blew out my bulbous thorax, somewhat pricked by his tone.

"Roger, isn't it?" murmured Ariadne, and as the wasp inclined his head with slight irony, she went on briskly, "Yes, I shall be taking him in with me."

Then she rose into the air and hovered there, flicking her tail. "No problem, is there, Roger?" she breathed, glancing down at the wasp.

"None at all," he said, and with a small smile playing about his segmented lower mouthpart, he ushered her through the broken windowpane. I prepared to follow.

"Out late, little fly," remarked the wasp. "Fancied a bit of dragonfly, did we?"

The way he pronounced the word *dragonfly* left me in no doubt as to his meaning. It was a scurrilous imputation—so I buzzed him.

"Brat!" hissed the enraged yellowjacket, his sting-charged rear end whipping upward like a scorpion's. I zipped at high speed through the laser-thin gap between the shards and the cardboard and swept abuzzing into the temple of the E(ROT)IC POTATO.

And was immediately stopped short in my trajectory by the sheer majesty of the spectacle that lay before me. Ariadne hovered near a moonlit rafter and, wordlessly stupefied, thrilled beyond language, I joined her. Together we gazed down from the high regions of its cathedral upon the splendor of the E(ROT)IC POTATO.

It was a dead man lying on his back under a table, with one hand on his breast and the other on a book on the floor. His chest had caved in and the hand itself had flopped limply into the cavity where once had been the heart. The heart itself, of course, was long since devoured.

And the man's eyes and ears and mouth and belly were alive with insects! And the space between his body and the table was filled with flying insects! And their sounds were amplified by the gabled roof and filled the gloomy chamber like the very drone of Eternity itself! And that vast booming buzzing harmony was a sonic articulation of the Triumph of the Insectile Will!

"Come, Gilbert," whispered Ariadne, and I followed her through the shafts of orange moonlight and descended with reverence deep into the bowels of the E(ROT)IC POTATO. There, in the darkness, I observed once again the milkwhite miracle of her ovipositor; but this time the organ was not withdrawn.

And then every dawning genetic tremor I had ever felt was finally fulfilled, not once, not twice, but a thousand times! A million times! A thousand million times! I quivered to the very quick of my being; I surrendered, fragmented, melted in the molten intolerable pleasure of it and dissolved to pure nonbeing, wrapped in shattering slithering Ariadne and sinking deeper and ever-deeper into the glow and pulse of the degenerating intestine of the E(ROT)IC POTATO.

LATER, STILL INTOXICATED, I LURCHED OUT, CREAMED and filmed with the eggy juices of insect love, and crawled away to lick my wings. The dull buzz of Eternity roared warmly through my drained and sated body, and I knew I was changed forever. As the moon sank to the horizon and the first brown rays of a new day probed the eastern sky, I knew I had finally become a fly.

Blood And Water

IMAGINE, FINALLY, A DIGNIFIED BRITISH BUTLER HOLD-
ing aloft a very large teapot and, followed by a serv-
ing maid pushing with some difficulty a tea trolley
containing cups and saucers and plates of cucumber
sandwiches, advancing the length of a smooth and
extensive lawn at the bottom of which flows a river,
and on the bank of the river a large weeping willow
tree, and in its shade six young people and an elderly
dame reclining in various postures upon tartan horse
blankets and swatting idly at the flies. It is August
1936, a cloudless Friday afternoon, and England is at
peace.

Now turn your eyes to the house which overlooks
the lawn, and see above the French doors giving onto
the terrace a woman standing at an upstairs window.
She is a pale woman in a white silk gown, utterly
motionless and devoid of expression, and she is gazing
out over the copse of chestnuts on the brow of the

distant hills, and into the deep blue sky beyond. There the tiny dot of a lone kestrel circles in the heat, dropping and rising as the currents dictate. It is at about this time, too, that a gray car comes into view at the end of the driveway in front of the house, shimmering in the heat and throwing up dust in its wake, and sounding at this distance like an insect. Just as the butler down by the river is pouring the seventh cup of tea, the woman in the white silk gown leaves off gazing vaguely at the distant circling bird and turns back into her room. It is on her account that an eminent Harley Street specialist named Gordon Cadwallader is alighting from the gray motor car which has by this time come to a halt in front of the house; without waiting for his baggage he passes through the front doors and is quickly spotted by the master of the house, who ushers his guest into the study off the entrance hall and closes the door behind them.

It is not until a few hours later, then, that we get our first clear glimpse of Dr. Cadwallader of Harley Street; and it comes as he rises naked midst billowing clouds of steam from his bathtub. Observe, first, the stoutness of the man. His chins and bellies are all pink and wobbly, and his great jowly buttocks dimple in the late sunlight as he gingerly lifts his hindparts and with enormous caution sets first one, then the other foot down upon the tiles. The head is large, bald save for a black mass of snaky curls about the ears, with small eyes set close together, a small bulbous nose, and a long drop from nose to lip. The bottom lip projects like the jaw of some cantankerous freshwater fish, and is flanked by overhanging flaps of flesh which pouch smoothly into the soft pink folds of the ample throat.

As he lifts his towel from the back of a chair and stands upright to dry himself, his breasts compose themselves upon the first swells of his gut like deflated cushions, wide, soft-nippled tires of flesh which but for the baldness of the man and the little pink hose-end of a penis peeping out from below would certainly identify the body as female. In the corner of the room stands an off-white, life-size statue of Minerva, goddess of plumbing, one outstretched arm snapped off at the elbow and Cadwallader's puce bathrobe draped over the stump. It is to this statue that the breasted physician now waddles, and taking up the bathrobe, he ties it loosely about his bulk. Pausing only to slip his feet into a pair of red Moroccan slippers, he tosses the damp towel onto his shoulder and steps into the corridor. As he does so, his air of scrubbed complacency is rudely jarred by a muffled explosion from somewhere deep in the bowels of the house; and a moment later he hears the distressed voice of an elderly woman cry: "Oh, Christ, Norman, there goes the bloody boiler again."

Now, the landed gentry is hardly prospering at this precise point in history, so when Cadwallader hears the boiler blow he is only too aware what it means. The house, Phlange, is a stately Georgian pile, and the Percy family has been there for generations. The plumbing system, unfortunately, has also been there for generations, and though Phlange's park of rolling meadowland is bisected by a branch of the River Kennett, its water supply is piped in from the reservoir at Newbury, some twenty miles away. The river is in fact used only for bathing, in the summertime, and skating in the winter; though skating has been forbidden since January 1928 when a small boy from the village fell through the ice and drowned. It was that same winter that the pipes froze, with the result that the following spring the cellars of Phlange were badly flooded.

All this is only too evident to the master of Phlange. He is Sir Norman Percy, a short, stocky, bad-tempered Roman Catholic gentleman with a thatch of yellow hair and bristling black eyebrows that meet on the bridge of his nose. When the boiler goes he is still in his study, going over the books and quietly grinding his teeth; as the sound of the explosion reaches his ears his head snaps up, and a most peculiar thing happens: A vein in his left temple, the one which twists from eye-level to hairline, suddenly stands out vivid and purple against the reddish skin and begins perceptibly to throb. At the same time a glazed look comes over the man's eyes and he rises to his feet with fists clenched so tight that the knuckles whiten to livid bonelike knobs. The truth of the matter is, for some months now Sir Norman has been subject to periods of sudden and intense disorientation, and occasionally he has heard voices. There is some history of madness in the family, and in his lucid moments he realizes he should probably see someone. For various reasons he has not; now, as the boiler explodes, some critical psychological strut snaps, and though you would hardly guess it but for the throbbing vein in his temple, Sir Norman crosses the thin line which separates the insane from the rest of us. But as I say, it is barely noticeable, this crack-up, and after a moment the aroused vein—a phenomenon known to psychiatrists and bartenders alike as "the snake"—subsides, and Sir

Norman goes off to fix the boiler like the good house-holder he is.

And what, finally, of his wife, of Lady Percy, the woman at the window? When the boiler goes, she, like Cadwallader, is emerging from a bathtub; but the profound depression that has been progressively enshrouding her mind is now such that the explosion causes barely a tremor to cross her unfurrowed white brow. She stands with her back to us upon the tiles and permits her maid to come forward and gently towel her pale body, the body which poses such problems for the men of Harley Street. She slips into her gown and then, like one entranced, moves across the bathroom and into her chamber, and her bathwater spins down the drain behind her with a swift, clear and noiseless motion. How different is the mood of the water in Cadwallader's bath! For there we find a scurfy vortex which makes horrible sucking sounds as it devolves and carries in its sluggish but implacable downward spiral a few hairs, a few crumbs of flaking plaster, and a number of small English insects.

WHEN THE DINNER GONG SOUNDS SIR NORMAN IS UNDER the boiler in his shirtsleeves and beside him is Tinkler, the estate handyman. They are deep in the cellars of Phlange, those drear crypts which still bear the malodorous and fungoid scars of the floods of '28. Dimly illuminated by a single naked bulb, the boiler room itself is a low-ceilinged vault of dank air and deep shadows, and dominating it like some great plated deity rears the cylindrical tank wherein the inner waters of Phlange are brought to boiling point and then forced to the upper regions by denser, colder water descending. The damage is less catastrophic than might have been imagined from the explosion; as usual, a matter of bad pipes, bad gas, and a moment of combustion vastly amplified by the emptied boiler. The thing can be patched up, of course, but clearly Sir Norman will soon have to have the professionals in, and extensive work will be necessary. The drain on his bank account—a leaky vessel generally as empty as this great rusting hulk of a water tank—is not to be thought of without deep dismay.

Eventually Sir Norman crawls out, closely followed by Tinkler, and the two men stand flaked with rust before the boiler. For a moment it seems, in its bulky rotting obsolescence, symbolic somehow of the end of all things, a great tinny membrane housing only a void; but no sooner has this thought occurred than Sir Norman dismisses it with a snort, and dropping a weighty spanner with a dull clang into Tinkler's toolbox, leads his man out of the barren and shadowy domain and into the light above.

POACHED TROUT WAS ON THE MENU THAT EVENING, BUT without Sir Norman at the head of the table the company lacked its binding agent, and things tended to fall apart. The Percy teenagers, Edgar, Gavin, and Charlotte, drank too much and squabbled loudly; Tarquin and Vanessa, the grown-up twins of Sir Norman's younger brother, the Honourable "Mad George" Percy, communicated only with each other, and in whispers. Roland Crub, a dissipated scion of the Northumberland

Crubs, read a book; and Lady Percy, fresh and sweet-smelling from her bath, sat silent and motionless at the foot of the table and ate nothing. Cadwallader, on her left, and Mrs. Crub, her mother, on her right, were so exclusively occupied with their food that little in the way of creative or exploratory discourse was to be had from either of them.

When the ladies had retired, along with all the young men, and the decanter of port had settled semiper-manently in front of the solitary Cadwallader, Sir Norman finally appeared, wiping his hands on a damp gray rag and cursing fitfully under his breath. Cadwallader watched him impassively, his little eyes betraying not a flicker of expression. Tossing the towel onto a side-board, Sir Norman took his place at the head of the table and poured himself a large glass of claret.

"Well," he said, having drunk, "have you thought about it?"

"Sir Norman," said the doctor, spreading his palms upon the table, "your wife is a very depressed woman. She must never be left on her own."

"Nonsense," snapped Sir Norman. "She's quiet, that's all. Always been quiet."

"On the contrary," murmured the doctor. "By all accounts she used to be a quite vivacious woman, until this curious deformity—"

"Never mind her deformity, Cadwallader," said Sir Norman sharply. "The point is, I absolutely forbid you to trumpet her condition to the world."

"A scientific monograph in the *Lancet* is hardly that, Sir Norman."

"I repeat, Cadwallader, I will not have her exposed to the idle gaze of strangers. That is final!"

From the depths of his great body the doctor produced a small sigh, and his long wet lower lip pursed briefly with irritation. While Sir Norman was being served his fish, Cadwallader had the opportunity to reflect that though he was used to dealing with the upper classes, used to their innate distrust of professionals and their obsessive need for privacy, he had never met resistance so nearly verging on the pathological as this man's. "I wish," he said, when the butler had withdrawn, "merely to provoke scientific interest in her condition. It is, after all, a rather unusual case of clitoral tumefaction—"

"Enough!" cried Sir Norman, and for the first time since the boiler exploded the snake was visible. "Hold your tongue, Cadwallader."

"Be reasonable, Sir Norman," said the fat man. "Medical science—"

"Medical science be damned!" continued the testy host, throwing down his napkin and rising from his chair. "You're the fourth bloody quack I've had down here, and instead of helping my wife all you can do is bleat about her suicidal tendencies while you further your own career at her expense!"

The butler reappeared and was brusquely waved away; Cadwallader, meanwhile, was visibly angered. His bulk stiffened and his lip trembled wetly. "How dare you impugn my integrity, sir!" he hissed. "If it were not for my patient's precarious mental state, I would leave your house this very minute."

Sir Norman's snake was now raging furiously. "Damn you, Cadwallader, and all your festering brood!" he shouted. "Leeches and parasites, the lot of you! I'll tell you something, Cadwallader"—by this time he was standing across from the doctor, leaning forward on his arms, palms down on the table, his eyes blazing madly at the pale Cadwallader—"you'll not have your way with her! She'll not go under your knife—not under any of your knives! Never, do you hear me, Cadwallader?"

With enormous effort the doctor gathered his dignity and rose unsteadily to his feet. "I must presume you are in liquor, sir," he said faintly. "I shall attempt to excise this unfortunate interview from my mind." And with that he fled, Sir Norman shaking his fist after him from the foot of the table, and roaring: "You'll not excise a damn thing in my house, Cadwallader, not a damn thing!" And then he slumped into a chair, breathing heavily, while the snake throbbed on like a wild thing in his temple.

IN THE POLICE RECORDS OF THE CASE, THE MOVEMENTS of every member of the house party over the next twenty-four hours are recorded in detail, along with all corroborating evidence. Cadwallader, it seems, spent most of his last day on earth dozing in a deckchair and sporadically working at the *Times* crossword. Old Mrs. Crub attended a harvest festival in the village, and awarded prizes for outstanding summer vegetables. Later, she took out one of Sir Norman's chestnut mares, and had a fine canter across the Downs. Her daughter spent the day in her chamber, apparently doing nothing till late in the afternoon, when a furious summer shower forced Cadwallader in from the garden to examine her; he found her condition essentially unchanged, and prescribed a powerful antidepressant.

The twins, Tarquin and Vanessa, were extremely vague about their whereabouts, and would say only that they'd been picking flowers in the woods. This did not satisfy the police, but by that time the outcome was clear, and the two were not questioned further. Roland Crub had motored into Newbury and spent some hours in a hotel room with a companion listening to a BBC broadcast of the Berlin Olympics. Sir Norman himself managed with Tinkler's help to get the boiler functioning, after a fashion, then gave his man the rest of the weekend off, but had him leave his toolbox in case further problems arose. He retired to his study, where, he said, he continued doing the books for a while, and then started to drink brandy. He drank steadily for the rest of the day, and on into the evening. He did not mention to the police that when the rainfall began he had seen a vision of his wife radiant in glory in the evening sky.

It seems that we can reconstruct the following sequence of events, beginning at or around 7:15 of that fateful Saturday night: Sir Norman, apparently normal but in fact profoundly intoxicated, makes his way to the east wing of the house with Tinkler's toolbox and slips unnoticed into Cadwallader's bathroom. He conceals himself in the linen closet and waits silently in the darkness as the doctor, sticky with perspiration after his day in the sun, enters and runs a bath.

We well know what Cadwallader looks like when he is at his ablutions. He is fat, and pink; and thanks to the recent efforts of Sir Norman and Tinkler he is once again privileged to wallow in hot water. The summer shower is over, and shafts of late sunlight slice through the steam, lending to the whole scene a rather spectral and fantastic appearance. Then the door of the linen closet slowly opens, and into this misty realm, this Avalon, this isle of the dead, slips the flaxen-haired knight. Gripped in his fist is a large spanner, and it glints in the sunlight as he advances unseen upon the back of his foe. Cadwallader, lost to the pleasures of immersion, sees nothing, hears nothing; Sir Norman lifts high the great steel tool, thin edge downward, and dispatches his man with one huge thump. Cadwallader doubles forward in the tub, then slips onto his side like some great vessel foundering in heavy seas, and the blood of his wound oozes out into the bathwater. Sir Norman does not pause to savor the joy of the kill, however; instead, he drags the toolbox to the bathtub and selects from it a fine-toothed fret-saw. Pausing only to roll up his sleeves, he goes to work.

Lady Percy, meanwhile, is in a state of nervous and spiritual exhaustion after being examined by the doctor, and she does not go down for dinner. She dismisses her maid, and then alone in her room in the west wing sits at her dressing table with a vase of blue columbines before her, compulsively arranging and rearranging the blooms. The hinged side mirrors of the dresser are set in such a fashion that the image of the woman and the flowers is reflected from one glass to the other and back again, and so on to infinity; and it is this movement of regression that first catches the eye of Sir Norman as he enters the chamber. In one hand he holds the spanner, and in the other a load wrapped in the black towel. Lady Percy sees him in her mirror and turns, rising to her feet with a small cry, and moves to the center of the bedroom. Her long white fingers are pressed against her lips, and her eyes are wide. Sir Norman stands stock still with his back to the door, and the two stare at each other across the wide chamber. His eyes burn with a manic fury; hers are vacant and ethereal. From the freighted black towel a quantity of blood drips suddenly onto the fine Turkish carpet. "Show yourself to me," whispers Sir Norman, crouching quickly to lay down his tool and his bloody load, his eyes never leaving her face. Lady Percy's hands move slowly from her lips to the clasp at the neck of her gown, and she deftly unfastens it. Behind her stands her four-poster bed, spread with a fine-woven coverlet of medieval design. Beyond the bed are the windows, and beyond the windows, arcing over the chestnut trees on the brow of the distant hills, a perfect rainbow has formed against the sky. Lady Percy drops her gown and stands before her husband, who falls to one knee. Her silver-blond hair is tied in a tight bun at the nape of her long white neck; her slim arms hang by her side; her skin is pale as ivory and her hips are narrow; and from the hairless pubis at the base of her flat belly sprouts a small, soft penis, plump and pinkly wrinkled, lying upon a delicate betesticled sac which hangs against her closed thighs like a rain-drop. Framed against the shimmering sky she stands there straight and pale and slender, and Sir Norman takes her hand and, lowering his head, presses her fingers to his lips. When he looks up, a flame of triumph glows in his fervent eyes. He opens out the oozing black towel and reveals the severed head of Gordon Cadwallader, its eyes yet open and blood dripping thickly from the ragged and truncated vessels of the neck. Now he snatches up the head by its black curls and raises it aloft before his wife's face; but the lady turns with a horrified shriek and flees to her bathroom, locking the door behind her.

Sir Norman, in deep psychotic territory at this point, becomes fascinated by the eyes of his enemy and, forgetting his wife, seats himself before the bloody head set between the mirrors on the dresser and there gazes into its infinite deadness. He is not aware of the water running in the bathroom; indeed he does not emerge from his gruesome reverie until he notices the bathwater which has come slithering, reddish and steaming, under the door and across the bedroom carpet like a serpent. His own snake is now quiet, and with a cry of anguish he dashes to the bathroom door and, finding it secured, batters open the lock with his spanner. When he finally bursts into the steam-filled bathroom, it is as he feared; his wife lies in an overflowing bath, her head lolling on the edge of the tub and her left wrist slit wide open with one of his own well-honed safety razors. Her blood drifts in misty swirls within the moving water, and Sir Norman, dropping his spanner, darts to the taps and turns them off with both hands. And then he lifts the pale dead hermaphrodite dripping from the water, and with a heavy step carries her into the chamber, and lays her on the bed. Gently he closes the eyes and, with the tears now rolling down his face, places her right arm by her side. The other he lets fall over the side of the bed and, careless of the blood still pumping softly from the wrist, presses the wound to his lips. It is then that some delicate atmospheric shift occurs in the air outside, and Sir Norman raises his head and sees, framed by the rainbow, a vast shimmering figure of light who slowly opens her arms and fills the sky with her radiance; and for a moment he is transfigured, and himself appears vividly aflame within her dazzling splendor. But only for a moment; and then the image dissolves, and darkness returns, and Sir Norman drops his head and presses his lips to the wound on the wrist of the corpse. And thus we leave him, as the gloom of twilight steals upon the chamber and the flies begin to gather on the doctor's eyes.

SOME TIME LATER, TWO VILLAGE POLICEMEN FOUND SIR Norman Percy kneeling at the bedside of his dead wife. They had been summoned by a chambermaid who'd come upon the headless corpse of Dr. Cadwallader floating in its own gore over in the east wing. Sir Norman offered no resistance, and the following day was arraigned at the county assizes at Newbury on a charge of capital murder. In a celebrated trial at the Old Bailey in the autumn of 1936 he was found not guilty by reason of insanity, and committed to Broadmoor Lunatic Asylum, as it was then called. After that first tragic blaze of psychosis had burned itself out, he resumed the role he had played so well all his life, that of the bucolic squire, and spent the rest of his mortal span, in Broadmoor, in a state of happy and imperious insanity. He died in 1957, and was buried beside his wife in the churchyard at Phlange. Upon his tombstone, curiously, is carved a verse of Melville, which runs:

What Cosmic jest or Anarch blunder
The human integral clove asunder
And shied the fractions through life's gate?

About the Author

PATRICK MCGRATH was born in England but now lives in New York City. His stories have been published in *Bomb*, *The Quarterly*, and *Between C&D*.